ALL OF US

THE SABELA SERIES BOOK 5

TINA HOGAN GRANT

Edited by Crystal Santoro Editorial Services: https://chrissyseditorialservices.org/

Cover Design by T.E.Black Designs – http://www.teblackdesigns.com

Visit The Author's Website

www.tinahogangrant.com

❀ Created with Vellum

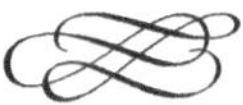

It was my idea, and now I was having second thoughts. I sat in silence while Slater drove on the way home, wishing I had discussed it with him first. I saw the look on his face when I brought up my spur-of-the-moment idea over dinner with our friends. His jaw dropping told me how shocked he was, yet everyone else at the table had misty eyes when they expressed how much they loved my idea and agreed to it. Looking back, I see now how I had put Slater on the spot. How could I have been so stupid? I felt terrible. Slater was the last to answer and had no choice but to say yes.

We were having dinner at one of our favorite restaurants to celebrate Travis's amazing recovery from his horrendous car accident that had left him in a coma for three days. He had just returned home after five weeks of rehabilitation. I had never been so scared in my life. We didn't know if he was going to make it.

Our closest friends joined us to welcome Travis home, his fiancée Claire, along with her parents, Jeffery and Abigail. Our son Scottie and my mom Charlotte were also there, and Jill with her new beau, Ricky. It almost felt like a reunion. I can't remember the last time we had a meal together, and it was great to see some of our parents meet for the first time.

The night's biggest surprise was after the dessert when Ricky and Jill announced their engagement. I was glad they waited until later in the evening to tell everyone and not steal Travis's night completely. But when they did, my emotions took over, and I blurted out without giving it much thought that we should have one big triple wedding since we were all engaged to be married.

At the time, it seemed like a beautiful idea, and everyone cried at the thought of sharing such a special day with close friends. I noticed Slater became extremely quiet after I pitched my idea, and immediately Jill started reeling off, how she wanted pink roses, and everything should be pink. Claire and I locked eyes for a second. Our eyebrows rose. Claire's facial expression told me she wasn't fond of pink either.

"Jill, not everyone likes pink as much as you do," I had said.

Jill looked at me with a creased brow. "But it's my favorite color, you know that."

Within minutes of making my announcement, I had already felt the tension. Jill acted like she was the only one getting married. She may have made many changes in her life recently, but the old Jill still has traits that continue to pop up, and this was one of those moments. I had to put her in her place.

"Jill, this isn't just your wedding. If we are going to do this, we need to make choices that we all like. I like pink, but I don't want everything to be pink at my wedding, and I sense Claire feels the same way," I said while making eye contact with Claire.

Claire nodded. "Sabela is right. We need to come together and plan this for all of us, not just what you like."

"And don't forget the guys. They are part of this wedding too, and they need to have a say as well." I added.

Rickey raised his hands. "I'm going to leave all the planning up to you, ladies. I'm okay with whatever you come up with," he exclaimed.

Travis quickly followed and raised his hand. "Me too." Have fun, ladies. I have no clue about any of this stuff."

I turned to Slater, who hadn't said a word since he had agreed to the idea. "What are your thoughts?"

He gave me a weak smile. "I'm still trying to let this all sink in, and you are already talking about colors."

From his stiff body and folded arms, I sensed that he was uncomfortable with a triple wedding. I realized then that it was wrong to mention it without talking to him first. After all, this was his wedding, too. I rested my hand on his knee and gave it a light squeeze. "Look, we haven't even set a date yet. We have plenty of time to get into the details and planning. It's Travis's night. Lets order another round of drinks and toast to his recovery."

For the rest of the evening, I tried to shake off Jill's remark that everything should be pink, but I just couldn't. In the back of my mind, doubt had set in. Was that a warning sign of how planning this triple wedding would be? I didn't want to jeopardize the friendship between all of us.

We are different in many ways and have been through a lot together. It has brought us closer together. I don't want to risk that.

Slater rested his hand on my shoulder, stirring me from my thoughts. "Hey, you are quiet. Are you okay?" he asked.

I sat up from the reclined position I was in and turned my head to look at Scottie in the back seat of the truck. I was happy to see he was sleeping. "Yeah, I guess."

Slater grinned. "I know that look. No, you're not. What's going on?"

I released a heavy sigh. "I don't know. I was wondering if this triple wedding idea is a huge mistake. I couldn't believe Jill when she said she wanted everything pink without even asking the rest of us. God knows how it's going to be when we start planning it."

"Well, it surprised me when you pitched us your idea. You've never mentioned a triple wedding plan with me before."

"I didn't have one until tonight. It just popped into my head, and I blurted it out without thinking." I took his hand and squeezed it. "I'm sorry, and I should have talked to you first."

"Well, it's too late for that now. It looks like it's full speed ahead."

"It's not too late to back out if that's what you want? I'm sorry I put you on the spot."

Slater shook his head. "No, I'm not backing out. Don't get me wrong, I like the idea, but a little warning would have been nice," he chuckled.

My spirits rose, "really. Do you think it's a good idea? What about Jill and her obsession with pink?"

"We both know Jill can be outspoken, and in the past, she has pretty much gotten what she wants. I know she's trying to change, but she has a long way to go," he joked. "All three of you girls have different tastes, and you are going to come to some bumps in the road where one of you is not going to like something." He cracked a laugh. "This wedding planning is going to put your friendship to the test. I'm with Travis and Ricky, and I'm leaving it all up to you three ladies."

I had to laugh at his comment. "You always know what to say. You are right about one thing; this will definitely put our friendship to the test. I just hope we can survive it. I don't want to lose Claire and Jill as friends."

"Then don't let it happen. If it means that much to you, then any conflict you encounter shouldn't be weakened by the bond you have together."

"But what if one of them or both ends up hating me? I can't control how they feel, especially Jill, who goes off the deep end sometimes." I slid back down into my seat and folded my arms. "Maybe I should just call the whole thing off? There is too much at stake."

"You will do no such thing. It's a brilliant idea and I, for one, am looking forward to it. I may not be able to help you plan it." He chuckled. "There is something scary about getting between three women planning a wedding." He squeezed my thigh and smiled, "but I'll try and give you any advice if I can. It's going to be okay. We've always said we are like family, and nothing can break that."

I released a heavy sigh and leaned back in my seat. "I hope you are right."

CHAPTER 2

It was after eleven when we finally arrived home. After putting Scottie to bed, I crawled into our bed and snuggled up close to Slater. My head rested on his bare chest, and the gentle sound of his heart beating in my ear soothed me. This was, without a doubt, my favorite time of the day. I considered it our time—a time when Slater and I could reconnect and feel close, with no interruptions from work and everyday life. I released a sigh and closed my eyes as I breathed in Slater's scent. "God, I love this time of day when it's just you and me."

Slater cupped my body with his arms and pulled me in closer. "It doesn't get any better than this—feeling your naked body up against mine."

I smiled with my eyes still closed. "Hmm, I have to agree. It was good seeing everyone together tonight, and I never thought I'd see the day when Claire and Jill would become friends."

"Well, let's see how the wedding plans go. That may change midway," Slater jokes.

"God, I hope not. It's Jill I'm worried about. You know how she can get if she doesn't get her way. I love her, don't get me wrong, but she got whatever she wanted growing up, from what I understand. Her parents spoiled her rotten. She once told me over lunch they were lawyers and never home. They traveled the world, taking on huge corporation cases. She told me they still send her a big check for Christmas every year."

"Wow, the way I look at it, one of you should be in charge. All these plans need a leader to direct and keep everything in order. Seeing how it was your idea, I think it should be you."

I raised my head and gave Slater a puzzled look. "You really think so? How do you think Claire and Jill will react to that? They might take offense to it."

"If they do, then I take back what I said, and we might want to reconsider doing this whole thing. It's like you said, you don't want to lose any friends in the process, and neither do I." Slater sat up and turned to face me. His face rested on the palm of his hand for support. "I think before you dive in, we all need to pick a date and be clear on finances. I think it's fair that we split all costs in three ways. The others are going to have to let us know how much they want to spend on this wedding, and from there, you ladies will have a budget to work with."

I gave him a loving smile. "Are you sure you don't want to help plan the wedding? I never thought of those two things," I laughed. "And without them, we can't begin planning." I threw my head back into the pillow. "Oh, what have I gotten myself into?"

Slater laughed. "I have no desire to be the only male planning a wedding with three women, but I'm here to give advice if needed." He squeezed my arm and gave me a soft kiss on the lips. "It's all going to work out just fine."

"What date did you have in mind?"

Slater leaned back. "Well, we have Thanksgiving and Christmas coming up in a few months. What about late spring, early summer of next year? Say early June?"

I did some quick calculations in my head and felt unsettled by his suggestion. "Yeah, that might work. It would give us ten months. I'll ask Claire and Jill."

"And by then, Travis should be much stronger and almost like his old self," Slater added.

"I'm going to call Claire and Jill tomorrow and tell them to discuss the dates with Travis and Ricky. Let's see what we can come up with in the next few days. Maybe I'll suggest we all meet at Claire's, so she doesn't have to leave Travis alone. Which she won't do, anyway."

"That's a good idea. Do Ricky and I have to be there? We have the Millers' house to finish."

I rolled my eyes. "No, you don't have to be there." I paused and smiled at him. "I sure do love you, and I'm going to plan the most beautiful romantic wedding."

Slater leaned in and rested his hand on my naked bosom before kissing me passionately on the lips. "I love you too, Sabela. You and Scottie are the best things that have ever happened to me. You are my world; I can't wait to call you my wife."

""Oh, Slater. You, Scottie, and I are all a family. Becoming your wife will complete everything." We kissed again. "Make love to me," I whispered.

Slater took me in his arms and pulled me in close. "You read my mind," he said before rolling his body on top of mine.

❧

The following day, I was eager to call Jill and Claire and get things rolling on the wedding plans.

After calling Ricky, Slater was out the door by seven, and little Scottie and I were in my truck by seven-thirty to drive over to his kindergarten school.

"Bye, Scottie. I love you."

"I love you too, Sabbie," Scottie said from his desk in his classroom. How I love the name he's given me. Only Scottie called me Sabbie. And because of that, he owned it, and it felt extra special to hear it roll off his tongue.

Back at home with a fresh cup of coffee steaming on my desk, I made myself comfortable and texted Jill, knowing she was at work.

Hey Jill, I'm super excited about our triple wedding. We need to come up with a date. If Claire is okay with it, do you want to meet at her place later this week and discuss how we are going to plan the wedding of the year? LOL.

I wasn't expecting a reply from her straight away and called Claire instead of texting because I knew she would be home with Travis. After two rings, she answered.

"Hey, Sabela, how's it going?"

"Good, thanks. How is Travis doing?"

"He's doing pretty good. It's great to have him home. Tilly is as happy as I am. She's all over him and won't let him out of her sight," Claire laughed.

"Aww, that's so cute. Tell him I said hi. Listen. The reason I'm calling is to see if Jill and I can come over this week and talk about wedding plans with you. We need to figure out a date so we can start planning."

Claire laughed. "That's a good idea. Travis and I were just talking about it over breakfast, and it's going to be such a special day for all of us."

"Have you talked about a date?" I asked.

"No. Honestly, it hadn't crossed our minds. Can you believe that? I'll talk it over with Travis and have some dates by the time we get together. How about the day after tomorrow? After Jill gets off work? Tomorrow, Travis has a doctors and physiotherapy appointment, and he's usually pretty tired when we get home."

"That works for me. I'll run it by Jill."

"Great. I'll order pizza."

"Sounds good. I'll get back to you soon, bye."

Sooner than expected, Jill texted me back, and I asked her about meeting at Claire's on Wednesday, and she agreed to be there at 5:30.

I was the first to arrive at Claire's. Slater left work early to watch Scottie, and was looking forward to his planned father and son movie night and hotdogs.

Claire looked comfortable in her navy blue sweats, bare feet, and a white tee-shirt. Tilly was cradled under her arm when she opened the door. "Hey Sabela, come on in."

"Hi." I held out my hand so Tilly could sniff it. "Hey, girl," I said as I gave her head a few loving pats. "She is so cute."

"And spoiled rotten," Claire added with a laugh.

Soft rock-and-roll music played in the background. I spotted Travis sitting outside on the patio. "How is he doing?"

Claire set Tilly down. "Go see daddy," she said in a playful voice, chuckling when Tilly bolted towards the open patio door. "He's pretty tired today, and they worked him hard at therapy yesterday. So we've just been hanging around here taking it easy." She laughed when Tilly sat at Travis's feet and barked—ordering him to pick her up, which he did.

"And how about you, Claire? How are you holding up? This has to be really hard on you."

"It's not as hard as when he was in the hospital. I honestly thought I was going to lose him."

"I know. We were all pretty scared. I'm so happy to see him home with you."

Claire folded her arms and stared at Travis. Love seeped from her eyes. "Yes, me too. He is my rock. I would do anything for that man. His attitude about this whole recovery thing has been pretty good. I wasn't sure how he would react to not being left alone or driving. But so far, so good. He tells me when he is tired and doesn't fight it. We've been watching a lot of movies, snuggling on the couch." She smiled at me. "The doctors said all his tests came back good. They want to keep him on the seizure meds for six months, just as a preventive measure. They said it's going to take some time for him to build up his strength and to take it slow and not rush into things."

"So no going back to work any time soon?" I asked.

Claire shook her head. "Well, we haven't discussed it in detail. It's just been a few days since he came home. But between you and me and advice from the doctors, he shouldn't be driving or working while on medication."

Her comment did not surprise me. "How do you think Travis will react to that?"

"I'm not sure. But everything is going well right now, and I don't want to upset him with the doctors' recommendations."

"Do you mind if I go out and say hi to him before Jill gets here?"

"No, of course not. Do you want a beer?"

"Yeah, that would be great," I replied as I headed over to the patio. "Hey Travis, how are you doing?"

Travis turned and looked at me and smiled. "Hi, Sabela." He petted Tilly as he spoke. "I'm hanging in there."

He looked weak and pale, and his weight loss didn't go unnoticed. "I'm okay. Slater says hi."

"Thanks. Is he managing okay?"

"Yes. Ricky has been a huge help and has been picking up a lot of the slack. Don't you worry about it? Just get well."

Travis nodded. "I'm working on it. So you ladies are going to discuss the wedding plans? It's a pretty neat idea you had. Claire and I are excited about the whole thing."

I gave him a caring smile. "Thanks. It's going to be a pretty special day for all of us, that's for sure."

A knock at the front door caught my attention. "That must be Jill. I'm going to go inside. Let us know if you need anything."

Travis nodded. "Will do. Thanks."

Claire quickly handed me a beer through the patio door opening, and then she dashed over to the front door. I took a large sip and entered the front room. Tilly raced past my legs, barking at a loud pitch, and greeted Jill with jumps and endless barks.

Jill knelt and picked her up. "Hey girl, I sure do miss you." She kissed her snout. "But it's because of you I now have a beautiful puppy called Maggie."

"Oh, you should have brought her over. I would love to have met her. She could have had a play date with Tilly," Claire said as she closed the door behind Jill.

"I couldn't; I came straight from work." Jill opened her jacket to show us her pink smock. "See, I still have my work garb on," she chuckled. "Ricky is heading home, and he'll be with her."

"So Ricky has moved into your place?" Claire asked.

"Sorta. He still has his apartment until the end of the month, and Sadie is still moving some of her things over to Logans. I still can't believe she eloped," Jill laughed.

Jill glanced my way to where I stood at the other end of the room. "Hi, Sabela," she said with a large grin.

I walked over to her and gave her a friendly hug. "Hey, Jill."

Jill beamed a huge smile. Something I had not seen in a long time. She was genuinely happy, and it showed. "You know your eyes light up whenever you say Ricky's name. It's good to see you happy," I told her.

Jill blushed. "Does it show that much? I'm sorry. I get so giddy whenever I think about him. It all happened so fast between us, but it feels so right."

"I know what you mean, Jill. When I first met Slater on the beach, I just knew he was the one."

Jill tilted her head and smiled. "Really? And you guys are so good together." She nudged my elbow. "And rich too, I hear."

"Jill!" Claire screeched. "That is none of our business."

I rested my hand on Claire's arm. "It's okay. I mentioned it to her at the hospital." I nodded at Jill. "We are doing okay."

Jill looked down at the beer I was holding. "Got any more of those?"

Claire ushered us over to the table. "Yes, let me go grab you one. Travis is on the patio if you want to say hi to him before we get started. The pizza will be here in about thirty minutes."

Jill looked out to where Travis sat with Tilly, now back on his lap. "He looks pale."

"Yes," Claire said, "he still feels weak. It's going to take some time for him to get his strength back."

"I'm going to go say hi. I'll be right back."

I nodded before taking a sip of my beer. "Sure."

Claire returned with two beers and set them on the table. "Have a seat," she said while glancing out at the patio. "Jill sure has changed, don't you think?"

"I'll say. I was just telling Slater last night what a surprise your friendship with her is."

"Tell me about it. I think no one is as shocked as I am, and I just hope it lasts."

"What do you mean?" I asked as I grabbed my bag with notepads and pens inside.

"Well, she changed after witnessing Travis's accident. I get that. But I hope a year or two down the road when the shock of it all is not so raw that she doesn't begin to revert to the old Jill."

"I hope not either, but she wasn't that bad. Spoiled, yes, and self-centered, but that's how I've always known her. This new Jill takes some getting used to," I chuckled.

Claire scuffed. "Speak for yourself. She was awful to me and even admitted how bad she treated Travis. I just hope she doesn't turn on us again."

"I honestly think she is all past that." I paused. "Claire, I didn't realize you were so skeptical about Jill. Are you sure you want to share your wedding day with her?"

Claire took a swig of her beer. "Oh yes, Travis and I both do. We talked about it when we got home and thought it was a brilliant idea. We are hoping this will only strengthen our friendship and erase any uncertainties that we may have of Jill," she chuckled. "Like my fear of her returning to the old Jill, and I think sharing a wedding may prevent that." She cracked a laugh." I mean how can she get mad at us after sharing our wedding day?"

"You have a point there. Slater and I also talked last night about Jill, and we, too, have concerns. I guess we feel the same way," I chuckled.

I glanced out at the patio and saw Jill turning around to re-enter the room. "Oh, here she comes."

I took another sip of my beer before pulling out my notepads and pens while Jill took a seat at the table and a swig of the beer Claire handed her. "Sorry guys, I didn't mean to keep you waiting." She glanced over at the notepads placed in front of me.

"You are going to take notes? You are so organized, Sabela."

I opened up a pad and checked to see if my pen worked. It did. "Yes, I figured I could keep track of all the planning and make any files if needed. I do it for Slater."

"Well, I do it at my work too for the patients," Jill whined. "Why should you be the one in charge?"

I rolled my eyes. The conflict had already begun, and we hadn't even started talking about the wedding. "Jill, I'm not in charge. No one is in charge. This is all of our weddings. I'm just going to organize whatever we plan so we don't forget anything. We will all have roles in the planning, and it's one of many."

Jill leaned back in her chair and folded her arms. "Fine."

I released a heavy sigh, relieved that she didn't want to pursue the matter. "Okay then. The first thing we need to come up with is a date. Did you guys talk to Ricky and Travis?"

Claire answered first. "Travis and I thought August would be good. It's the hottest time of the year, and if it's going to be a beach wedding, the temperature should be perfect."

"I like your choice better than mine and Slaters. We thought about mid-June, but you are right. We've had some cold days in June."

"Yeah—June gloom, we call it. When the marine layer doesn't lift all day," Claire said. She turned and looked at Jill. "What do you think, Jill? Did you and Ricky decide on any dates?"

"I was hoping for a Valentine's Day wedding, that would be so romantic." Jill gushed with dreamy eyes.

"Jill, that's only four months away, and we need more time than that. Especially with Thanksgiving and Christmas coming up," I barked. "And besides, February is always cold."

Jill didn't fight back and surprised me when she answered. She slumped back in her seat. "Damn it, you are right. February is cold. I hate the cold. August would be much better, I agree."

I raised my hands in triumph. "Great, we are getting somewhere. August is the month, and now we need to narrow it down to a day. Any suggestions, ladies?"

Claire spoke. "Well, it should be on the weekend, and I'd prefer a Saturday."

"I agree," I said while bringing up the calendar on my phone. "That narrows it down a bit."

Claire and Jill mirrored my actions and looked at the calendars on their phones.

"Well, our choices are the 5th, 12th, 19th, or 26th." Claire read from her phone. "Those are all the Saturdays in August," she added.

Feeling I had been a little rough on Jill, I asked her first. "Any of those dates pop out for you, Jill?"

Jill looked at her phone. "How about the middle of the month? The 19th or 26th? Either is good for me." She looked over at Claire. "What about you, Claire?"

Claire continued to look at her phone. "Eeny meeny miny moe."

Both Jill and I laughed. "Well, that's one way to pick a date," I said.

After finishing her rhyme, Claire looked up and smiled. "August 19th."

I gave a stiff nod. "Sounds good to me. August 19th will be our wedding day."

Jill clapped her hands. "Wow. This time next year, we will all be married. Can you believe it?"

I leaned back in my chair. "Ever since Slater proposed to me on the beach over two years ago, I've been dreaming of our wedding. And now that we have Scottie, it will be even more special."

"Do you think you and Slater will have kids of your own?" Jill asked. I saw the guilt in her eyes when she glanced over at Claire. "I'm sorry, Claire. I didn't mean to bring kids up."

Claire gave a forced smile. "It's okay, Jill. Just because we can't have kids doesn't mean I should deny you two from talking about them."

"That's very noble of you, Claire. I confessed. And I haven't said anything because I've felt uncomfortable talking about kids around you."

Claire sat up in her seat and took a swig of her beer.

"What's going on, Sabela?"

"Yeah, Sabela, what's going on?" Jill echoed.

"Well, a few months after we got Scottie, I stopped taking the pill." I beamed a smile. "Slater and I are trying to get pregnant."

Jill and Claire's eyes lit up, Jill gasped. "No way! Are you serious?"

"Wait, are you trying to tell us you are pregnant?" Claire interrupted.

"I'm not sure. I'm three weeks late." I broke out into a smile.

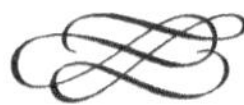

CHAPTER 4

*J*ill's eyes almost popped out of her head. "Holy shit! Have you ever been late before?"

I shook my head. "Never. I've always been like clockwork."

"Does Slater know? "Claire asked.

"Not yet. I want to be sure before I say anything to him. When he mentioned a June wedding, I didn't know what to say because if I am pregnant—I will still be carrying the baby or about to give birth any minute." I cracked a laugh. "Imagine if I went into labor on our wedding day?"

"Oh god! That would be just our luck too," Jill joked, softening her tone. "Wow, I can't believe you are gonna be a mama."

"Now slow down. I'm not sure yet. We tried to get pregnant so that Scottie would have a brother or sister. We didn't want to put it off any longer. He is growing so fast." I turned to Jill and gave her a hard stare. "Jill, promise me you won't say anything to Ricky. He works with Slater every day, and I don't want him to say anything to him. If I am, I want Slater to be the first to know, and I want him to hear it from me."

Jill looked offended by my request. "I'm not going to say anything," she snarled.

I detected some sadness from Claire when she spoke and maybe a little jealousy. "Yeah, you don't want too much of an age gap between them. That makes sense." She took another swig of her beer. "I'm happy for you guys."

I smiled. "It's not official yet. I'm going to buy a test this weekend." I paused and tried to erase some of the guilt I was feeling. "You know, Claire, we are still hoping you and Travis will be able to run the foster home someday. It's just gotten delayed because of Travis's accident. But Slater still plans on looking into it and seeing what needs to be done to make it happen."

"Thanks. I know that. Slater mentioned it at the hospital."

"Good. I just don't want you to think we had forgotten about it."

The buzzer for the main entrance to the building startled us. Claire got up from her seat. "That must be the pizza." She glanced out on the patio. "Look at that. Travis and Tilly are sound asleep." She walked towards the intercom and buzzed the pizza man in.

Jill looked at me, leaned back in her chair, and folded her arms. "You know, I bet you are pregnant."

I released a nervous laugh. "Why do you say that?"

"Because you have that glow about you. I've seen it in pregnant women that have come to the dentist's office. You have that same glow with rosy cheeks." She nodded. "Yep, I bet you a hundred bucks you are pregnant."

I dreamed of having Slater's baby ever since I stopped taking the pill and only felt disappointed when my period arrived on cue every month. In my mind, I was hoping Jill was right. But this month, it did not, and every day that passes brings me to expect that Slater and I may finally be pregnant.

The smell of pizza filled the air, and I suddenly had an appetite. "Do you need any help, Claire?" I called her in the kitchen.

"Nope. Just going to grab some paper plates and napkins. I'll be right out."

Jill stood up. "Let me come grab the pizza," she said as she walked towards the kitchen.

A few minutes later, they appeared with everything we needed to feast on pizza. I looked out on the patio and saw Travis was still sleeping. "We should save him some."

"Yeah, I'll put a couple of pieces aside," Claire said as she set the pizza box in the middle of the table.

After taking a few bites, I continued with our wedding discussion. "Okay, so we have a date. We need to come up with a budget. How much do you want to spend? We are not planning a huge wedding, right?"

Claire took a swig of her beer. "Our money is going to be tight for quite some time with Travis not working. And not only that, we are getting medical bills for what our insurance didn't cover. If it's going to be on the beach, I'm assuming it won't be that expensive."

I nodded, and then Jill spoke. "I hope we are going to have some kind of party afterward? It's our wedding day, and we need to celebrate."

I glanced over at Claire. "Well, we can't have alcohol on the beach, but we could have a reception at one of the nearby restaurants."

Jill clapped her hands and squealed. "I love that. We can have a DJ and dancing, oh and lots of champagne."

I laughed at her excitement. "Yes, we can, Jill. What do you think, Claire?"

"It all depends on the cost. I'm sure my parents will help, but I can't go crazy."

I smiled. "Slater and I can help too. But I agree. Let's not go overboard." I made a shortlist in my notepad. "Look, I have no idea how much any of this stuff will cost. Right off the top of my head, I'm thinking of our wedding dresses, the men's wardrobe. Decorations for the beach. The reception, flowers, invitations, to name a few. I'm sure there will be more." I had a thought. "What do you think about going barefoot? I can't see us wearing heels on the sand, and besides I like to feel it between my toes."

"Brilliant idea," Claire and Jill echoed.

"We will need to get our hair and makeup done, a photographer, and a cake," Jill chirped."

"Oh yes, a cake! I didn't think of that," I replied, running some numbers through my head. "How does $5000 each sound? If we go over, Slater and I will pay it."

Jill smiled. "That's a good number. I will get my check from daddy at Christmas so that I will be fine."

We both looked at Claire, anticipating her reply. She was quiet.

"Claire? Is that too much?" I asked.

"No, that sounds reasonable. We both have some savings, and like I said, I'm sure my mom and dad would love to help."

I turned to Jill. "Are you going to invite your mom and dad? And what about Ricky's parents?"

"Yeah, I'll invite them. I'm not sure if they will come through? They are too busy enjoying the good life in Spain," she joked.

Claire repeated my question. "What about Ricky's parents?"

"I'm not sure. I'll have to ask Ricky. He has a sister too. She lives in Los Angeles, and they haven't seen each other in over three years. I hope she comes. I would love to meet her."

"Oh, I hope so too. I never knew he had a sister. He never talks about her." I said, surprised by the news. "I'm sure my mom is going to want to be involved with the wedding planning, which I would love," I added. "Are you both okay with that?"

"Mine too," Claire laughed. "It's fine with me, Sabela. I love your mom. She was so sweet over dinner when we celebrated Travis coming home. She made me cry when she started crying over your suggestion to have a triple wedding." Claire took another sip of her beer. "Do you think your parents will want to be involved?" Claire asked Jill.

Jill waved her hand. "Oh, hell no. They will probably make an appearance on the day of the wedding and then, knowing them, head back to Spain the next day."

I looked at my list. "So, what do we want to tackle first?"

"I want to buy my pink wedding dress," Jill cried out loud.

I rolled my eyes. "Jill, I thought we had already told you that Claire and I do not want a pink wedding."

"Well, I didn't think you were serious. You know it's my favorite color."

"But it's not ours. Again, I felt like I was being harsh with Jill, but there was no way I was going to have a pink wedding. If you really want a pink wedding, then maybe you shouldn't get married with us."

"Well, that's not fair," Jill moaned. "How come you two have a say in the colors, and I don't."

Claire took control of the conversation. "Look, let's talk about the colors at a later date. Maybe we can work something out. Don't you think we need to find out if we need any permits for holding a wedding on the beach? They may take a while if we do."

"Good Idea," I said while adding it to my notes. "I can take care of that?" I had a thought. "Hey, I was thinking of having the wedding at the point where the huge rocks jagged out next to the Fisherman's Grill. The scenery is stunning?"

Jill and Claire looked at each other and nodded. "I love that spot," Jill said.

I was relieved to hear Jill was not going to dispute my idea.

"Me too!" Claire added. Travis and I have taken many walks there."

"Fantastic. It's where Slater and I first met." I said with a smile. "Hey, do you two want to check out the restaurants and see how much a reception would cost? There are at least five that I know of."

"Won't they need a headcount?" Claire asked.

"Yeah, probably, but we can get a rough idea."

"I'm in," Jill said. "Do you want to start this weekend, Claire?"

"As long as Travis can go with us. Remember, I can't leave him alone."

"Oh, that's right. Sorry, I forgot. That's fine with me."

"And we can't be gone too long. He gets tired easily and will need to come home and take a nap." She released a heavy sigh. "I hate to be a drag, But Travis is my number one priority right now. Everything I do revolves around him."

My heart went out to her. "Claire, there is no need to apologize. We are all in this together. Travis's well-being is our priority too. When he is ready to go home, you just let Jill know."

Claire's eyes suddenly showed sadness. "You know, the wedding is only ten months away, and I don't even know if Travis will be up to an all-day wedding celebration."

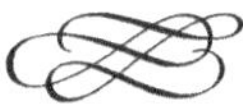

CHAPTER 5

After leaving Claire's place, I took the scenic route home along the Pacific Coast highway and pulled off to where the wedding would be.

I turned off the engine, rolled down my window, and filled my lungs with the ocean air. I don't know what it is about the ocean, the breeze, and the sound of the waves crashing against the shore, but it always brings me peace no matter what is going on in my life. I stepped out of my car and started over at that point. It was prominent where the land jolted out and met the ocean with jagged rocks and a flat plateau on top.

Claire, Jill, and I stood side by side, looking into our future husbands' eyes. Visions of our wedding clouded my mind. I smiled at the thought before removing my shoes and throwing them in the back seat of the car.

The sand felt warm between my toes, and I dug them deeper into the cooler sand as I walked across the beach. Oranges, reds, and yellows painted the sky as the sun had set on the horizon. "God, what a beautiful night," I said out loud. I hope it's this beautiful for our wedding.

Memories flooded my head from when I first met Slater. It was on this beach almost three years ago. He stole my heart the minute I spotted him checking me out. I had just left Davin at the airport after saying our final farewell. But he soon became a distant memory when I locked eyes with Slater.

I giggled when I spotted the secluded cave off in the distance. It was where we first had sex and allowed strangers to watch us. It was out of this world, and man, what a rush. Since we got custody of Scottie, we haven't done anything as adventurous as that, and I'm not sure if we ever will again. Oh, but our fantasies are just as good.

I breathed in the salty air and closed my eyes. The warm wind brushing through my hair and across my cheeks was liberating. When I opened my eyes, I looked out to sea and saw there were still a few surfers and swimmers and a couple of sailboats coming in. The water must be warm. People scattered on the sand, lying on towels; some sat in lounge chairs while they ate, and others strolled the shoreline with their feet in the water.

The beach has always been one of my favorite places, and I couldn't think of a better place to become Slater's wife. I smiled at the thought and headed back to my car.

I found Slater and Scottie curled up on the couch when I arrived home. A bowl of popcorn rested on Slater's knee, and Scooby-Doo played on the TV. My heart melted at the sight before me—my family, my world, and soon to be my husband and stepson. Life couldn't get any better. The volume on the TV was set at a child's level. Higher than what we adults could handle, and they hadn't heard me come in.

After quietly setting my purse on the bench by the front door, I tiptoed across the room. "Got room for one more?" I asked with a huge grin.

Slater looked up and matched my smile. "Sabela, I didn't hear you come in." Scottie was engrossed in his movie and never looked up. Slater gave his arm a nudge. "Hey, Scottie, scoot closer to me and let Sabbie sit down."

Finally, Scottie acknowledged me and smiled as he scooched closer to Slater. "Hi Sabbie," he said before filling his mouth with popcorn.

I took a seat next to him and squeezed his side. "Hey champ, good movie?"

With his eyes glued to the TV, he nodded. "It's funny."

I looked across at Slater and stretched my arm behind Scottie to reach for his hand. He smiled. "How did it go?"

"Great, we are getting married on August 19th."

Slater beamed a huge smile, and his eyes sparkled. "Really, what happened to June?"

"We all decided that August was much warmer, and it would guarantee us a sunny day, unlike June, where we sometimes have those June glooms."

"You have a point, smart thinking. So do you think you ladies are going to be okay planning the wedding together?"

"Yeah, Jill whined about a few things, but she soon came around after Claire, and I reasoned with her. She's still insisting on a pink wedding, though, which Claire and I honestly don't want."

"Make that three," Slater laughed. "I'm sure Travis and Ricky will feel the same way. It looks like we outnumber her on that one, and I wouldn't worry about it."

"Yeah, but it's her wedding, too. She may have been dreaming about a pink wedding ever since she fell in love with the color, and that could have been years ago. She's always had an obsession with pink since I have known her."

"Yes, but she has to realize it's not just her wedding. She has to be willing to make some sacrifices."

"That's what I told her. She didn't take it too well, but Claire quickly changed the subject and said we would discuss colors later. I can't tell you how thankful I was for her to butt in and take over.

If she hadn't, I had a feeling Jill and I would have gotten into a big argument."

Slater squeezed my hand. "I'm sure you will come to a solution where everyone is happy. Don't overthink it. It will come to you."

I released a sarcastic laugh. "Ha, that's easy for you to say." I reached in front of Scottie and patted Slater's knee. "Enough about Jill; I'm going to soak in the bathtub while you two watch your movie." I gave Slater a wink. "After I have put Scottie to bed, we can continue this conversation in the bedroom."

Slater's eyes lit up. "I like your plan."

CHAPTER 6

From the comfort of our bed, I watched and admired Slater. He undressed and slipped under the covers, sliding his body close to mine.

"Damn, I'm a lucky man," he whispered before embracing my naked body and giving me a long sensual kiss on the lips where I found his tongue and savored the taste.

"Not as lucky as me," I chuckled and pressed my body against his, wrapping my arms around his neck. "I love you so much."

Slater smiled, rested his hand on my breast, and kissed me again. "I love you too."

I felt his manhood stir against my upper leg and gave him a cheeky grin as I reached down and took it in my hand. "What do we have here?" I giggled as I stroked his shaft in my palm.

Slater rolled back and closed his eyes, giving me complete access to his now prominent erection. I pulled back the covers and circled my lips with my tongue. "Hmm," I moaned as I continued to slide my hand up and down his manhood with long, forceful strokes before taking him into my mouth.

Slater released a loud moan and pushed down on my head so I

would take him completely. "Oh yes," he cried, while raking my hair with his fingers. "You have no idea how good that feels."

I raised my head and laughed. "And you have no idea how good you taste." I resumed the position of my mouth over his shaft and worked my magic with my tongue and massaging hands. Slater met my rhythm and within minutes came, flooding the back of my throat with his juices.

"Damn, girl," Slater gasped between breaths.

I laughed as I wiped my mouth with my hand and fell back to the pillow next to him. "Tomorrow night will be your turn." I winked.

Slater chuckled, "Deal, my soon-to-be wife."

I smiled. "Only if the three wives to be can pull off the wedding plans in time and don't kill each other in the process."

"Hey, if you need help, let me know, okay?" Slater said in a more serious tone.

I sat up and patted his thigh. "As a matter of fact, you can help me with something, but it has nothing to do with the wedding."

Slater joined me by sitting up and creasing his brow. "What is it?"

"Travis and Claire."

He creased his brow again, and his upper lip curled when he spoke. "Travis and Claire? Are they okay?"

"I'm not sure. After talking with Claire about the wedding costs, I got the impression they are struggling, not a little, but a lot. Claire is too proud to let me in on all their finances. She told me that their money was tight, and I understand that, with Travis not working. He will get a little from disability, but nothing like he did when he worked for us. Basically, Claire is the one supporting them."

"What are you asking, Sabela? Do you want me to give them some money?"

I shook my head, "Not without getting something in return."

"Sabela, you are not making any sense. What are you trying to say?"

"The foster home. You still want to do it, right?"

"Well, yeah, but Travis is nowhere capable of running it right now. He has to get well."

"I know that, but before we can even open the doors to children, we need to do a lot of research and footwork to find out what we need to do to make it happen."

Slater nodded. "True, but we have no time right now. I have some big jobs coming up, and you are planning our wedding plus helping me run our business."

I smiled, "but Claire could."

Slater grinned. "I see where this is going. You want me to hire Claire to do the footwork?"

I nodded and matched his grin. "Yes. We could pay her much more than what she is making now, and she can do most of the research and phone calls from her home. Which means she could still take care of Travis."

I could tell Slater liked my idea. He straightened his back and spoke with enthusiasm. "Didn't she say that she would quit her job to do whatever it takes to make the foster home plan happen?"

"Yes, when we first told them our idea. That was before the accident."

Slater leaned forward and kissed me on the lips. "Sabela, you are brilliant. Let's invite them over for dinner this week and see what they think."

"That's a great idea! I'll call Claire tomorrow." I hesitated. "Should I tell Jill?"

Slater furrowed his brow. "Why should we tell Jill?"

I shrugged my shoulders, realizing how stupid I sounded. "Never mind, I just don't want her to get mad at me. She got upset with me at the hospital because I hadn't said anything about the foster home. She makes it sound like we are doing stuff behind her back."

"You're kidding? We don't need Jill's permission for anything. This doesn't concern her. Why does she always think she has to be included in everyone's business? I like Jill, but damn she gets under my skin sometimes."

"She's always been that way. It's the one thing I don't think will ever change about her. You are right. This is none of her business. I'm not going to say anything. If Claire wants to, that's her decision."

Slater nods. "Good call."

I chuckled. "But be prepared when she finds out. I'm sure she will have a few words for us."

Slater made himself comfortable beneath the covers where I spooned him. "I'm ready," he said in a firm voice.

"You better be," I whispered before closing my eyes.

CHAPTER 7

After returning home from taking Scottie to school, I spent the morning scheduling some estimated appointments and going through paperwork that we've had sitting since before Travis's accident.

By one o'clock, I was free to call Claire and grabbed my phone. After three rings, she answered.

"Hey, Sabela. What's up?"

"Hey Claire. Slater and I were talking last night, and we had an idea that we wanted to propose to you and thought we could do it over dinner at our house."

"Is everything okay?" Claire asked, sounding worried.

"Yes, everything is fine. It's about the foster home."

"I thought we put that on hold for a while because of everything that has happened." She went silent for a moment, and then I detected the sadness in her voice. "I would understand if you decide to go with someone else. There would be no hard feelings."

"Claire, that would never happen. Let the four of us have dinner, and Slater and I will tell you our ideas."

"Could we meet at our place?" Claire asked. "The fewer places I have to take Travis, the better. He gets tired so quickly."

Guilt swept through me. "Yes, of course, but I don't want you fixing dinner for all of us when you have Travis to take care of."

"Then bring dinner with you," Claire replied, followed by a chuckle.

Her answer made sense, and I could have kicked myself for not suggesting it. "You got a deal. How about this Friday?"

"Sounds good. Travis gets up from his nap around four and will be alert to listen in. Does 4:30 work?"

"That works for me, see you then."

"Come on, Sabela, we are going to be late." I heard Slater call from downstairs.

"Hold on a sec; I'm putting on Scottie's shoes," I hollered back. "I still have to grab the lasagna from the counter that is cooling off."

"I'll get the food and meet you in the truck. I'll text Claire and let her know we are running late. It's almost 4:30 now."

I continued to struggle with Scottie's shoe as I tried to squish his foot into it while he stiffened his foot and curled his toes. "Okay, I'll be right there." I turned my attention back to Scottie. Putting shoes on a kid was not easy—especially one that couldn't sit still. "Scottie, be still. We have to go. Daddy is waiting."

Since Scottie came to live with us, I soon discovered that being on time for any appointments was almost impossible. Even if I got ready earlier, I have yet to make it anywhere on time. Getting Scottie ready was a chore and a game to him. He'd play tag or hide and seek and take his time picking out toys for his bag.

We arrived at Claire's thirty minutes late, and Scottie immediately made friends with her dog, Tilly.

"You need to get him a dog," Claire laughed as we stood in the middle of the room, watching him being chased by Tilly.

"Oh god, no, I have my hands full with him."

Claire leaned in. "Maybe one more," she whispered. "Do you know yet?"

I shook my head and scanned the room. Slater was outside on the deck with Travis. "No, I'm buying the test tomorrow," I whispered back.

"Call me when you know."

Slater and Travis entered the room, and I gave her a quick nod.

"What are you two ladies talking about?" Slater asked as he and Travis took a seat at the table.

I lied, "dinner. Claire and I are going to go dish it up while you two men catch up and keep an eye on Scottie."

I followed Claire into the kitchen. "Show me where your plates and silverware are, and I'll set the table while you dish up the lasagna."

Claire opened a drawer with the silverware and a cupboard door with plates inside. "Here you go."

I grabbed a handful of silverware. "So, are you and Jill going to check out some restaurants tomorrow?"

Claire reached up and placed five plates on the counter. "Yes, Jill has called a couple already, along with The Fisherman's Grill, which is the closest to our spot. They told us to come by at four after the lunch rush."

"Great, I called about permits, and we need one, so I filled out the application online. It takes about fourteen days."

"Awesome, I'll call you tomorrow after I get back from the restaurant."

"Sounds good. Let me go set the table."

I left Claire to dish up dinner and found Slater and Travis in the middle of a conversation about work.

"How's Ricky working out?" Travis asked Slater.

"He's doing well. We have a big job starting in a few weeks, so Sabela is going to be hiring a crew."

"Wish I could help, man. Soon I should be able to come back. I'm feeling pretty good."

Slater glanced my way and gave me a worrisome look. I matched his stare and then returned to the kitchen. "How's it coming?" I asked Claire.

"It's all dished up. This looks good. You made this?"

I blushed. "With the help of Stouffer's, it's a family-size frozen lasagna and bakes in the oven for an hour." I glanced at the oven. "How is the garlic bread doing?"

"It should be ready by the time we get these plates on the table and Scottie away from Tilly."

After helping Claire with the plates, I called Scottie over to the table. "Aww, but Tilly and I are playing."

"You can play after dinner. Now come on, let's eat."

Scottie let out a moan in protest. "I don't want to."

Slater butted in with his firm male voice, which has been needed more often lately. "Scottie, listen to Sabbie. It's time to eat."

I tried to hide my giggles as I watched Scottie moan again and walk to the table with his arms folded and his shoulders hunched over. "I'm not hungry," he said as I pulled out a chair next to Travis.

Slater raised his voice a notch. "Enough, Scottie."

Travis stretched his arm around the back of Scottie's chair and leaned in. "Does that mean I can have your plate, too? I'm starving."

Scottie giggled. "No."

Travis looked across the table and threw me a wink. I loved watching him toy with Scottie. He was a natural with kids. "But you said you weren't hungry," he said in a playful voice.

Scottie threw back his head and giggled again. "I was kidding."

"Aww, man, so I can't have yours."

Scottie shook his head and laughed. "Nope, it's all mine."

Slater and I shared a smile. I sensed he was thinking the same thing I was. Travis would be great with the kids in the foster home. Sitting next to Scottie, Travis was glowing. There was no denying he loved kids.

Claire joined us at the table and filled her plate with two slices of pizza. She took a bite before speaking. "So, what did you two want to talk about?"

I glanced over at Slater. "Do you want to tell them?"

He leaned back in his chair and gave Travis and Claire a caring smile. "We wanted to talk to you about the foster home."

Travis shifted in his seat. "Hey man, I'm sorry if I'm holding you up with your plans. As soon as I'm back to normal, I still want to run the place with Claire." He took Claire's hand. "If you still want us."

"Of course, we still want you, but Sabela and I thought we could hire Claire now to do all the research and footwork. There's a lot of it, and Sabela and I don't have time. Claire may have to take some classes also, which we will gladly pay for."

Travis creased his brow. "Are you asking her to quit her job and come work for you?"

A worried look smeared Slater's face. "Well yeah, she wouldn't be able to hold down both jobs, and we know money is tight for you, and we are willing to pay her much more than what she is making now."

Travis gave Claire a sharp look and curled his lip. He snarled at Slater. "I don't want your charity. This is temporary. I'll be able to provide for us soon."

Claire stroked Travis's arm. "Calm down, honey. They are just trying to help."

Fearing this may get into a heated discussion, I turned to Scottie. "Hey sweety, do you want to go eat on the deck with Tilly?"

His eyes grew wide. "Can I?"

I laughed at his excitement. "Sure."

Scottie grabbed his plate in a flash and called Tilly, who obediently followed with a wagging tail. Together, they left and claimed their spot on the chair outside.

Slater immediately defended his words. "Travis, it's not charity. I'm offering Claire a job, and once you are physically able, I would like to hire you, too. But you have to concentrate on getting well. That is a priority for you."

"So I guess Ricky has taken my place on the job sites?" Travis asked with a hard stare directed at Slater.

"For now, yes, and to be perfectly honest, seeing how you bought it up, I'm not even sure you could ever do construction again. Which is why the foster home will be good for you."

"So you are firing me?"

Claire rubbed his arm again, "Travis, stop."

Travis pulled away from Claire's hold. "No, I want to know. Tell me, Slater, are you firing me?"

I felt unsettled by Travis's tone and tried to shift the mood. "He's not firing you, Travis. He is just being realistic."

Travis raised his voice and leaned forward, locking his hands together as they rested on the table. "Shut up, Sabela. I didn't ask you."

Slater matched his tone. "Hey, now hold on a second. Don't tell her to shut up. She's right. I'm being realistic. No one knows if you will ever regain your strength one hundred percent, and if you do, we have no idea how long it's going to be. It may take six months or a year. In the meantime, I have a business to run."

"Well, if you don't want me back, I call that, firing me."

Slater leaned back in his seat and threw down the pizza that he held. "Oh, come on, Travis. You know damn well. If I could take you back right now, I would, but I can't. No doctor is going to give you a pass to work on a construction site, and I wouldn't allow it either," he paused. "Which is why we want to move forward with the foster home, and we can if we hire Claire."

Travis shook his head, narrowing his eyes. "You have no idea how this makes me feel, Slater. I should be able to take care of Claire. I don't want her supporting me."

"And you will, as soon as you are well enough. Like I said, this is just temporary. A way to get things rolling on the foster home."

Travis folded his arms across his chest. "Then why does it feel like charity?"

Slater shrugged his shoulders. "I dunno, man; Claire can work where she works now or work for us for much more money. It's a job offer—plain and simple. We even talked about it before the accident. What's changed? You didn't call it charity then."

"What's changed is I had a damn accident that almost killed me and left me where my fiancé has to wear the damn pants in the household, and I'm fucking sick of it." Travis beat on his chest. "This is not me. I hate being this way."

Claire grabbed his arms. "Stop it, Travis. That's enough."

Travis pushed her away and stood up away from the table. "Stop treating me like I'm an old man, Claire. I want my life back, and I want to take care of you."

Tears bellowed in Claire's eyes, and my heart went out to her. The pain they both felt was undeniable.

"Do you want us to leave?" I asked in a soft tone. "We can talk about this another time. There is no rush."

Travis shook his head. "I'm done talking. Do what you want. You don't need me."

With a push of his hand, he shoved his chair away, and I watched as it fell to the floor. Without looking back, Travis stormed into the bedroom and slammed the door.

<h1 style="text-align:center">CHAPTER 8</h1>

I looked with pity across the table at Claire, who refused to make eye contact with us from embarrassment. Instead, she looked down at the table and wiped the tears that were running down her cheeks. I didn't know what to say. I'd never seen Travis so hot-tempered and short with his words before. After a few moments of silence except for the sounds of Claire's sob, she finally spoke.

"I am so sorry. He didn't mean it. For the past few days, he has had these terrible mood swings. One minute he is the Travis we all know and love, and then the next, he is mean and short-tempered. Just like what you saw."

"It's okay, Claire. You don't need to explain," I replied in a soft voice.

"I'm sure it's the after-effects from the coma," Slater said as he took my hand.

Claire nodded. "It is. I called the doctor this morning when he was sleeping. He gets upset over the stupidest things. When I last saw you, I thought he was doing well. But as each day goes by, he gets impatient and wants to be strong and fit like he used to be. But it won't happen overnight, and I keep telling him that."

"What did the doctor tell you?" I asked.

"He said it's normal to have mood swings, but there is no telling how long they will last." Her tears became heavier. "This is so hard. I feel like I'm walking around on eggshells in fear I may piss him off. He wants to be independent and gets angry when I try to help him and he tells me I'm smothering him. He doesn't get it, that he can't be left alone. It's too soon. They say he is at a high risk of having a seizure."

The sliding glass door that led out onto the deck interrupted us. Scottie walked in with his empty plate. "I'm all done," he said with triumph.

I smiled and hugged him when he handed me his plate. "Good boy, now why don't you take your bag of toys to the front room and show Tilly."

He looked at me with his sweet grin that always melted my heart, "good idea." He turned and waved his hand at the dog. "Come here, Tilly."

Once Scottie was settled, Slater started up our conversation again. "It's obvious to me he has low self-esteem and feels worthless. I feel foolish that it didn't even occur to me when I mentioned hiring Claire."

Slater's remarks stunned me. "Slater, none of this is your fault. You were only trying to help them."

"I'm not saying it was, but what I was thinking? First, I tell Travis that I don't need him at S & S construction and doubt that I ever will, and then I ask Claire to work for us and exclude Travis from the whole idea. He has every right to feel useless."

"That makes a lot of sense, but Claire said he has had frequent mood swings. It's not just about what happened a few minutes ago."

"He has," Claire confirmed.

Slater nodded. "Yes, because he has to rely on Claire to be here and watch him. He's not handicapped. He does normal things like us. But he can't drive, work or make a paycheck. He has to rely on Claire for everything. That can do a guy in."

"You are right, Slater," Claire said with sad eyes. "And I don't know what to do about it."

Slater leaned back in his chair and folded his arms. "We have to approach this differently."

"What do you mean?" I asked.

"Well, first of all." Slater stared at Claire as he spoke. "Do you want to work for us?"

"Yes, of course, but not without Travis, and he doesn't seem to want to. It was our dream together."

Slater moved his forefinger up to his mouth. "That's because I never asked him."

Claire creased a brow. "Yes, that's because he can't work right now. He's too fragile."

I was just as confused as Claire was. "What are you getting at, Slater?"

"What if we make Travis feel needed? Include him in the research that has to be done."

Claire shook her head. "Travis is terrible on the computer. He doesn't even know how to send an email."

"But you do, Claire," Slater said, giving Claire a nod as he spoke.

"Well yeah. I'm the one that pays all the bills online and keeps track of our bank accounts."

"So why not do it together? Let Travis sit next to you while doing the research and filling out the necessary forms. I'm assuming most of it can be done at home. The bottom line is we need to make Travis feel needed."

"I appreciate your ideas, Slater, but that still doesn't take care of the fact that he can't drive, be left alone, or earn a paycheck. I'm not sure if it's going to help."

"I think the pity he feels for himself will subside once you involve him in the work you are doing. The urge to be alone will soon go away if we keep his mind busy. Don't you agree?"

"Yeah, I can see that," I answered, "But what about a paycheck and not driving?" I added.

"Well, I can't fix the inability for him to drive. That is a safety and medical issue, and he just has to accept that. As far as a paycheck goes, well, we can pay him something in cash each week so he can still keep his disability, and it will make him feel like he is contributing to the household."

I smiled and rubbed his thigh. "I love the ideas you have."

Claire sat up with hope in her eyes. "You would do that?"

Slater chuckled at her sudden mood change. "Well, it's not charity, as Travis put it. I expect him to work for it. And it would be up to you, Claire, to make sure he does. Give him some tasks. Show him how to use the internet and do some research."

Claire waved her hand. "Oh, he knows how to look stuff up. It's the forms and tedious things that he can't do."

"Well, it's time to teach him. Sabela had to show me how to run the books. I'm glad she did. She keeps track of them most of the time. But there are days where she has appointments and is running all over the place, and I will sometimes take care of them."

"I can do that," Claire said with a half-smile.

Slater smiled, "I know you can. And I'm sure there will be days you will need to go to the foster house and talk about ideas. Take Travis with you. The bottom line is, we need to boost his self-esteem, and together I know we can."

I looked at Slater with such admiration and rubbed his knee. "You always have the best ideas."

"Well, let's see what Travis thinks." He turned and looked at Claire. "Do you want to get him and see if we can convince him we need his help?"

Claire nodded and picked up the chair Travis had knocked over before heading to the bedroom.

A few minutes later, she returned with Travis trailing behind her. I noticed straight away that Travis avoided eye contact with Slater and me as he took a seat next to Claire. This might be more difficult than we had all anticipated. I knew how stubborn Travis could be, and I was seeing it now.

Slater spoke first. "Are you doing okay, Travis? We didn't mean to piss you off."

Travis kept his eyes fixed on the table. He folded his arms. "Yeah, I'm okay. What's up?"

"Well, after you stormed off, I talked with Claire, and she said she can't do everything on her own when it comes to the foster home, so she is going to need some help."

Travis looked up and gave Slater a hard stare. He shrugged his shoulders. "So, what are you telling me for? I'm no use."

"Why do you think that, Travis? Because you can't drive or work on the building sites?" Slater asked him. His voice was stern.

Travis rolled his eyes. "Yeah, why do you have to keep reminding me? Is that why you called me out here?"

I butted in. "Just listen to what Slater has to say."

Slater continued. "Travis, the work that is needed does not involve any kind of construction. We had already finished the house, and you were a big part of it. Yes, Claire will have to do the driving when you go there, but that's temporary. It's just a safety measure. What did the doctors tell you? Six months that will go by in no time."

"So, what are you saying?" Travis said in a flat tone.

"Claire is going to need help getting the necessary permits and licenses that are needed to run the place. She needs to do a lot of research and work with agencies that place foster children in homes. It's a lot of work for one person. You guys can work as a team. She needs help, Travis."

Travis shrugged his shoulder again. "I don't know how to do any of that stuff."

"Nor do I, Travis. We can learn together." Claire told him, startling us with her suddenly raised stern tone. "You need to stop feeling sorry for yourself."

Travis snarled at her. "I don't feel sorry for myself, Claire."

Claire cut him off. "Let me finish, okay, and yes, you do feel sorry for yourself. You mope around here like it's the end of the world. Do you even realize how lucky you are to be alive? I thought I was going to lose you. I was afraid you would wake up a vegetable and not know who I was. But look at you, Travis; you are functioning. You have very minimal side effects, and each day you are getting a little stronger. So what if you never do construction again. It's a hard way to make a living, anyway. Your dream has always been to foster a couple of kids. Well, here it is being handed to you on a silver platter." Tears pooled in her eyes as she reached for Travis's hand. "For three days, Travis, I waited by your bedside in the hospital for you to wake up, and I'm here at home day in and day out, helping you get well. I was and always will be here for you, and now I need you." She squeezed Travis' hand and pleaded with him. "Don't let this opportunity for the both of us slip away because of your stubbornness. I also want this, but I won't do it alone. I can't do it alone. Like Slater said, this is the perfect time to do all the necessary paperwork, research, and classes if needed while you are recovering."

Travis remained silent, taking in everything that Claire was telling him. A few times, he nodded, but he said nothing. Slater and I held our breath as Claire did her ultimate pitch. This was her break it or make it moment. She had a way with words, and I could tell she was getting through to him, from his rigid posture that was now relaxing and the moments where their eyes locked.

After a few minutes of no words from Travis, Claire prodded his thoughts. "What do you say, Travis? Are you in? I could use your help. Don't forget I'm planning OUR wedding with Sabela and Jill, which is another reason I need help. I can't do all this alone."

He raised his head slightly, glanced our way, and spoke directly to Slater. "And you would pay me for doing a bit of paperwork?"

Slater leaned in and narrowed his eyes. "It's not just a bit of paperwork. It's a lot, and it would mean spending hours on the phone and probably many trips to the house to discuss plans. So yes, I would pay you and in cash, I might add, so you can keep your disability, and like Claire said, she's going to be busy with the wedding plans, too. That's a lot for one person."

He turned to Claire, taking her hands and raising them to his lips. "It has been a dream of mine, and to share it with you would be another dream come true." He smiled. "Let's do this."

Claire beamed a big smile. "Really?" She hooked her arms around Travis's neck, where they met in a kiss. "Oh Travis, you won't regret it. I promise. I'm going to call work first thing in the morning and tell them I quit."

Emotions ran high at the table while Travis and Claire embraced in a kiss. Slater and I hugged while he gently wiped a tear from my cheek that had escaped.

"Welcome aboard, Travis," Slater said while still locked in my arms. I think this is just what you need to feel better about your future."

CHAPTER 9

The next morning, shortly after nine, Claire called me with the good news that she quit her job. It did not surprise me when she told Dr. Larson. He took it well in his usual pleasant manner and told her to keep in touch. I was also pleased to hear that she told Jill before being connected to Dr. Larson's office. Jill squealed on the phone about how excited she was for her and Travis.

"So you told her everything?" I asked. "I mean about coming to work for us and running the foster home?"

"Yes, I said I was quitting so Travis and I could start getting the foster home up and running. She was super excited for us."

"Thank you for being upfront with her. The news relieved me, and I didn't need another Jill meltdown right now. I was happy Claire told her. It wasn't our place to tell her. Now there will be no surprises for Jill. Slater and I had discussed whether to tell her, but we decided not to do that.

Claire laughed. "I learned the hard way not to keep things from Jill. And besides, I have a deeper respect for her. She is trying hard to change her ways and has come a long way. We are meeting up later after she gets off work to check out some restaurants. I'll let you know how it goes."

"Great, I can't wait to hear what you found out."

After ending the call, I got back to my paperwork and confirmed over the phone some estimates scheduled for tomorrow. It would be a full day, which meant the only time I could go to the store alone was today if I wanted to do the pregnancy test this weekend. I checked the time on my phone. I had to pick up Scottie in two hours and decided to go before picking him up.

At the store, I was overwhelmed by the variety of choices for a simple pregnancy test. I had no idea there were so many different brands. I didn't want to rely on just one—what if it was defective and opted to buy three different brands and use them all?

After purchasing them, I sat in my car, holding the brown bag in my lap. It suddenly seemed so surreal that I may be pregnant. I had the sudden urge to race home and do the test immediately, but I quickly talked myself out of it. I wanted to be in the right frame of mind and take my time, making sure I was doing it right.

Slater will be taking Scottie to T-Ball Saturday morning. That would be my golden hour to find out our fate. I made the excuse that I needed to get some work done and would have to stay home. I knew in my heart that if I were not pregnant, I would need time to overcome the immense disappointment I knew I would feel. I pleaded with myself all week that I am carrying Slater's baby.

After picking up Scottie and arriving home before Slater, I left Scottie in front of the TV to stash the tests in my dresser drawer before Slater got home.

Holding the tests in my hands, the thought that I may be pregnant raced through my mind constantly. I couldn't shake it, and if I were, I would plan something special to break the news to Slater.

It warmed my heart when I thought about how his reaction would be, and then I thought of Scottie. How would he react if we told him he was going to be a big brother? I tried not to have such thoughts because it would be such a huge let-down if I were not. I loved having these dreams and hoped they would all come true.

Saturday couldn't come soon enough. I had a restless night, tossing and turning, wondering about the test results. I came so close over the past few days to telling Slater that I might be pregnant, but I didn't want to get his hopes up.

I raced around the house, getting Scottie's things together for his T-ball game. I packed them lunch and some extra cold drinks before ushering them out the door. "Go on, go. You don't want to be late."

Slater stopped at the front step and turned. "You sure you don't want to come? You can always do your work later."

I had to think of an excuse fast. "I can't—I have a few scheduled conference calls."

Slater creased a brow, "On a Saturday?"

"Yeah, it was the only time they could fit me in. I'm sorry. I'll catch the next game." Looking over Slater's shoulder, I saw Scottie was already waiting by the truck. I waved. "Bye, Scottie; I love you."

Scottie waved back and yelled. "I love you too, Sabbie."

Slater leaned in and gave me a tender kiss on the lips. "You work too much. We will miss you, and I'll see you this afternoon."

My hands rested on his chest. "I'll see you then, bye."

I watched as Slater pulled out of the driveway and blew kisses to Scottie as he waved, wearing a huge grin. God, I love that little boy. Once they had turned the corner, I took a deep breath and went back inside. The time had arrived.

Not wasting a moment, I raced upstairs and grabbed the tests from the dresser and was about to head to the bathroom when my phone rang from the bedside table. "Damn it." I questioned whether to answer it and decided I would decide after checking the screen. I saw it was Claire and released a heavy sigh, knowing I would have to take the call. My first thought was something may have happened to Travis.

I disconnected the phone from the charger and paced the room as I answered. "Hey, Claire, what's up?"

"Hi Sabela, sorry I didn't call you last night. Did Jill call you?"

"No, is everything okay?"

"Yeah, I think so. We checked out some restaurants yesterday. Fisherman's Grill, which is the closest to the beach, has some great menus and prices, but Jill started talking pink again, and I kind of went off on her. We need to talk to her about this. I'm not having a pink wedding, Sabela."

I rolled my eyes. I didn't want to get into this right now. "Can we talk about this another time? I'm kind of in the middle of something right now."

"Well, can you at least give Jill a call and tell her straight up that there is not going to be a pink wedding? She won't listen to me. She started asking the guy at the restaurant if they had pink napkins and tablecloths. Yuck! She got upset when I laughed and said no pink at my wedding."

My patience was growing thin. "Claire, I'm super busy. I'd much prefer we discuss colors when we are all together. Let's figure out a time to meet next week. I really have to go."

Claire's tone turned flat. "Fine, but don't forget Travis and I have a meeting with you on Monday to discuss the list you put together for the foster house."

I rolled my eyes again. "Yes, I know. I have you scheduled for nine in the morning. I'll figure out another day for us to meet with Jill. Now I really have to go."

"Okay, we will see you on Monday. Will Slater be there?"

"Yes, he will be joining us. I'll talk to you soon, bye."

I ended the call in haste and shook my head as I grabbed the brown bag and headed to the bathroom. "Friggin Jill, she can be such a pain," I mumbled as I closed the door and removed the tests from the bag.

After reading the instructions carefully on each box, I saw they all followed the same guidelines and would show results within five minutes. They were the longest five minutes of my life as I paced the bathroom floor, listening to the ticking clock on the wall countdown each minute.

I gasped when I checked the one on the left. "Oh my god, it's showing the two lines, which means pregnant." I raised my hands to calm myself. "It may be a faulty test. I need to wait for the other two." My eyes raced back and forth between the two remaining tests. "Come on, hurry up," I shouted as I looked closer for any signs of a result. Then I saw them. Two more positive signs appeared. "Oh, my god." My jaw dropped as I raised my head and gazed at my reflection in the mirror. "I'm pregnant. Slater and I are going to have a baby, and Scottie is going to be a big brother."

CHAPTER 10

I was shocked and exhilarated all at the same time. My legs felt weak at the knees, and out of fear of falling, I pulled open the door and taking comfort of my bed, where I sat on the edge and rubbed my belly. I can't believe I am pregnant. Slater and I are going to have a baby. Tears pooled in my eyes at the thought. I flopped back on the bed and giggled with joy. My heart was complete, and I had the urge to pick up the phone and tell someone. My mom immediately popped into my head. I can't wait to see her face when we tell her she is going to be a grandma. "Oh, daddy, I wish you were here to meet your grandchild," I whispered as I continued to caress my belly. As much as I wanted to tell my mom, I needed to tell Slater first.

I sat up and laughed when I saw I was still rubbing my stomach. The thought that another human being was growing inside of me was mind-boggling. Was it a boy or a girl? I laughed again. I didn't care, and I'm sure Slater won't either. Scottie, I'm sure, would prefer a little brother. I pictured him playing big brother and smiled.

I grabbed my phone and saw I had a few hours before they

returned from Scottie's game. I didn't want to just tell Slater about the baby. It needed to be a momentous occasion that he would never forget. I headed downstairs, grabbed an iced tea, and went and sat on the patio to rack my brain for ideas.

Within five minutes, I had an idea and raced back upstairs with my phone and grabbed one of the pregnancy tests I left on the bathroom counter. I checked my face in the mirror, smiled at my reflection before holding up my phone and showing my sweetest smile as I took a selfie. I have never been keen on taking selfies, but at that moment, I felt radiant, and my face was glowing from knowing I was going to be a mom.

After taking the picture and tossing the tests in the brown bag and then into the trash bin, I headed to the office, where I printed out the selfie I had just taken. "Not bad," I muttered. I then wrote a note using a black marker on a piece of paper, which I folded in two before taping the selfie to the front. I held it up and laughed and slid it into a white manila envelope and wrote on the front of it. With the envelope in my hand, I hurried downstairs into the kitchen and checked the top of the fridge. I smiled when I saw we had a pack of rolls, also known as buns.

Giggling at my plan, I checked the time and knew I didn't have time to bake a cake. Instead I opted to pick one up from Ralph's Bakery and be back home before Slater and Scottie returned.

Once home from the store, I wrote my special message on the top of the cake with an icing pen and then hid the cake in the fridge. With everything in place, I was giddy and couldn't stop smiling. Since discovering I was pregnant, I felt nothing but pure bliss. I was marrying the man of my dreams and having his baby. Life couldn't get any better.

Lost in my thoughts, I had lost track of time, and the sound of Slater's truck pulling into the driveway brought me back to reality. A mixed rush of panic and excitement raced through me as I anticipated them coming in. I wanted to act natural and scowled in the kitchen for something to do.

Three minutes later, the door opened, and Scottie raced through the front room to the kitchen, where I was wiping down the counter. I checked the oven, and I could feel the heat.

"Sabbie, I hit the ball three times," Scottie yelled as he ran into my arms.

"That's great, buddy. Give me a high-five."

Slater came in a few minutes later carrying Scottie's bag and the ice chest. "Hey, babe. You should have been there. You would have been so proud of our boy," Slater said after freeing his hands of the gear and giving Scottie a triumph pat on the head.

"I wish I could have been, but I had business to take care of."

Slater stood by the stove and folded his arms. It was exactly where I wanted him to be. "So, how did it go?" Slater asked as he leaned back against the stove.

"Oh, good, it was an eventful day," I said with a grin.

Scottie took a seat at the table and grabbed an apple from the bowl, and dug his teeth into it while swinging his legs back and forth where they dangled from the chair.

Slater leaned forward and touched the top of the stove. "Did you know the oven was on?"

"Oh yeah," I reached across the counter and handed Slater an oven mitt."

"Can you take it out? I just turned off the oven before you got home."

Slater took the mitt and turned around. I couldn't help but notice his perfect backside as he bent over. "What are you cooking?" he said as he opened the oven door and pulled out the single bun.

He turned to face me, his brow creased. "A bun?"

I gave him a flirtatious smile as I walked towards him. "Yup, a bun in the oven."

"That's all you are having for lunch? A single bun?"

"I thought we could both enjoy a bun from the oven." I released a subtle laugh. He hadn't put two and two together. I tilted my head and gave him a tender kiss on the cheek.

Slater looked at the bread he still held in his hands. "Are we on a diet?" he joked before setting the roll on the counter.

"Oh, I don't mind if I gain a few pounds over the next few months."

"You will if you can't fit into your wedding dress."

I gave him another kiss. "I'm sure I'll lose it by then." I took his hand and led him over to the table. "Why don't you sit down with Scottie."

As soon as he sat down, he saw the white envelope and picked it up. "What's this?"

My stomach churned with nerves, "Oh, a little something from me."

Slater inspected the envelope, front and back, before reading the writing on the front out loud. *"Do you know what you are?"* He looked up and grinned. "What's this?"

I took a seat next to him and rested my hand on his thigh. "Open it."

"But it's not my birthday," he said as he slid his finger under the flap.

"It doesn't have to be for this."

Slater gave me a puzzled look as he pulled out my homemade card. I waited as he took it in, and then I saw his eyes light up as he read the words on the card. "No!" He read my words out loud. *"You are going to be the best daddy to Scottie's little brother or sister."* He studied the picture. He looked at me, his eyes bright. "Is that a pregnancy test?"

"Yes, sweetie, I'm having a baby. I'm pregnant."

Slater's jaw dropped, and his eyes remained wide. "You're pregnant? Oh my god, Sabela. We are having a baby?"

I nodded and leaned in, locking my arms around his neck. "Yes, we are."

Slater looked at me with dreamy eyes before kissing me

passionately on the lips. "I love you so much." Then he laughed. "Now I get it, a bun in the oven."

I matched his laugh and slapped his chest. "Took you a while."

Slater looked over at Scottie, who was oblivious to our conversation, and instead inspected his apple closely after taking another bite.

Slater spoke to him in a soft voice. "Hey buddy, how would you like to be a big brother?"

Scottie looked at his dad with a puzzled look, "Me?"

We both laughed, "Yes, you. You are going to be a big brother. Sabbie is having a baby."

Scottie cocked his head to one side as he tried to process what Slater told him. "And I will be his brother?"

"Well, we don't know yet if it's a boy or a girl, but yes, you will be the brother—the big brother."

A big grin appeared on Scottie's face. "Cool. I'm going to be a big brother."

Slater stood from the table and laughed as he knelt beside Scottie and wrapped him in his arm. "That's right, buddy. And you are going to be the best big brother."

Suddenly, I remembered the cake and opened the fridge. "It's time to celebrate and have some cake."

Scottie's eyes lit up. "We have cake!"

I giggled as I pulled the cake out of the fridge and set the box in front of Slater. "Open it," I said as I went to grab a knife.

Together Slater and Scottie opened the cake box, and Slater read the words I had iced on top. "*I can't wait to meet my daddy and brother.*"

Scottie squealed. "That's me; I'm the brother."

Slater and I laughed as I sat on Slater's lap and hooked my arms around his neck. "I love you."

Slater stared into my eyes before kissing me. "I love you too, mommy to be." He then pulled back and gave me a hard stare. "Hey, wait. Are you going to be pregnant at our wedding?"

I shook my head. "No, if my calculations are correct, the due date is sometime in June."

"Wow, that's cutting it close. Good job, we didn't go with a June wedding."

"Does anyone else know you are pregnant?"

"No, I wanted to tell you first, which reminds me. I've been dying to tell my mom. You thought she was excited about the wedding. Wait until I tell her she is going to be a grandma." I scanned the room. "Where's my phone?" I spotted it across the table. "Scottie, hand me my phone," I asked with my hand out.

I put the phone on speaker, and after three rings, my mom picked it up. "Hey, mom, it's Sabela."

"Hi, sweetheart, is everything okay?"

I smiled at Slater as I spoke. "Everything is great. What are you up to? Are you home?"

"Yes, I just sat down with my dinner, and I'm going to watch Scrubs reruns. I love that show."

"Oh good, you're sitting down. Slater and Scottie are here, and we have some news for you." I saw Scottie was about to speak, and I quietened him with a finger to my mouth. Afraid he would spill the beans.

"Oh, what is that?" Charlotte asked in a worried tone.

I took Slater's hand and squeezed it. "I'm pregnant. You are going to be a grandma," I shrieked, with tears running down my cheeks.

My mom's squeals of joy were so loud I had to hold the phone away. "You're pregnant! You are going to have a baby?"

Slater laughed. "Yes, Charlotte, Sabela is pregnant. It's due in June," Slater said, beaming a large smile.

I heard my mom sniff back her tears. "I need a tissue. I can't stop crying. Oh, I wish your father was here."

"I do to mom, but he is watching over us."

"So much is happening—the wedding and now a baby. This is so exciting. I love you two so very much."

"We love you too, mom. Why don't you come over to Claire's this week when we discuss wedding plans. I'll let you know when and what time as soon as I find out."

"I would like that. Thanks, now you have to take care of yourself and watch what you eat. You have a baby to think about now."

I rolled my eyes. It had already started. "I will, mom. We are going to celebrate with some cake. Love you."

After ending the call, I remembered Jill's obsession with pink and wondered if my mom would have a way to reason with her and drop this idea of a pink wedding.

CHAPTER 11

The following day, when the house was quiet with Slater at work and Scottie in school, my work in the office was interrupted by an overly excited phone call from Jill.

"You're pregnant! I knew you were pregnant. I just knew it."

I laughed out loud. "Yes, you are right. I'm pregnant. Boy, news travels fast. How did you find out?"

"Ricky just texted me. Slater told him at work. I'm so happy for you guys. I'm going to be an auntie."

I laughed again and questioned her reply, "You are going to be an auntie?"

"You betcha, Auntie Jill, I like that. Oh, I hope it's a girl. Do you know yet?"

"No, I have no idea. I haven't even been to the doctor yet. I just took the test yesterday and told Slater and my mom."

"Oh, I bet your mom is over the moon. Wait a second!"

"What?"

"We are going to have to have a baby shower. Wow, so much is going on—the wedding and now a baby shower."

"Also, the foster home. Slater wants to work on that too. I don't know how we are going to pull all of this off. The baby is due in June. I hope I have an easy pregnancy so I can help with everything."

"Oh, I'm sure you will be fine. You are one healthy mama. Now, as soon as you know the sex, you gotta let me know so I can plan the baby shower."

Her gesture touched me. "You would do that? That's really sweet."

"I'm Auntie Jill, remember. It's what aunties do. Hey, I gotta go. I'm at work. We will talk soon."

"Okay, bye." After I had hung up, I envisioned a baby shower planned by Jill, if it's a girl. There would be no escaping a pink overload. God help me.

Slater and I met with Travis and Claire on Monday as planned, and it went really well. Travis seemed in a much better place than when we had last seen him and was eager to learn and help Claire with whatever tasks we threw at them.

"So when is your last day at the dentist's?" I asked Claire after we wrapped up the meeting.

Claire shuffled her notes and placed them in a folder. "Well, I have this week off with pay, but I told Dr. Larson; I'm not coming back after my vacation is over."

"How did he react?"

"He was actually pretty nice and wished us luck on our new adventure." She looked up and smiled. "Hey, how are you feeling? I can't believe you are pregnant."

"I'm doing good: no morning sickness or anything. I hope it stays that way." Guilt suddenly swept through me. "Hey, I have to ask, but are you both okay talking about babies and my pregnancy? I hope I'm not making you uncomfortable?"

Claire shrugged her shoulders and looked at the floor. Her body language told me it did, but Claire was too polite to hurt my feelings. Travis answered for them.

"We don't have a problem with it. We see pregnant people every day at the store and when we are out and about."

"Yeah, but you don't know them or talk to them. This is a little different. I just don't want to upset either of you."

Claire spoke this time, "Sabela, it's okay. We are fine. I'm truly happy for you. I admit I'm jealous, but what you and Slater have done for us with the foster home certainly helps with our woes. We've had so many late-night conversations in bed about the home and the kids that we will be helping. We share ideas and what we want to do to make the children feel loved. Plus, we are as excited about having a big family when the home opens as you are about your baby."

I released a huge sigh of relief. "Aww, that makes me happy," I chuckled. "Oh, and get this, Jill wants to plan the baby shower. She will love it if it's a girl."

Claire let out a loud laugh. "Oh, no! Maybe she will get over her pink obsession with the wedding if she does a pink theme at the baby shower."

"Oh, heck no, not Jill." She wanted a pink Christmas tree this year, but Ricky soon put a stop to that."

Claire glanced across the room and saw Slater and Travis were now in a deep conversation. "Hey, when do you want to meet next to discuss the wedding?" She asked me.

"I was hoping for this Friday. Tomorrow I have my first doctor's appointment for the baby. My mom would like to join us on Friday."

"Great! I'll invite my mom and dad too. They are anxious to help."

"What parents aren't," I joked.

"Jills'." Claire quickly answered.

She was right. I had forgotten about them. Jill rarely spoke of them. "You are right. I wonder if they will come to the wedding? Jill doesn't see them too often."

Claire shrugged her shoulders. "I hope so. They sound like they are enjoying life in Spain. I wonder who Jill takes after?"

"I'm guessing her mom," I replied.

Slater approached us and smiled. "I have to get back to work. Ricky is holding down the fort."

"Okay. I'll see you tonight." I told him and watched with pride as he left the dining room where we sat.

Travis joined Claire and me at the table.

"We should get going, too, Travis. You have to be at physiotherapy in an hour."

Travis nodded. "Yeah, I know. I'll be glad when this shit is over with."

"You look like you are doing great, Travis. You've come a long way." I told him.

"Yeah, if I had it my way, I'd just get on with life and be done with all these doctors and their crap. But Claire won't let me."

Claire rolled her eyes. I sensed they had already had this conversation before. "Oh, don't start, Travis. You are worse than a ten-year-old. And you are making it much harder on me with all your whining."

Travis raised his voice a notch. "What the fuck are you talking about, Claire? Harder on you? I'm the one doing all the work and restricted from doing anything. Give me a frigging break."

Claire matched his tone. "Just for a few more months, Travis. What's the big deal? I'm sick of arguing with you over this." She turned to me and shook her head. "I'm sorry. We go through this every day. I'm just as anxious as he is for all of this to be over." The sound of the front door slamming shut startled us. Travis was gone. Claire grabbed her jacket from the back of a chair and threw it over her arm. "God damn him. I'm sick of his friggin mood swings. I gotta go before he takes off again."

"Take off? He's done that before?"

"Yeah, yesterday. I found him sitting on a bench at the park, feeling sorry for himself. I'm not sure how much more I can take.

We will do the work for the foster home, but I didn't want to say anything in front of him. But I don't want to rush into getting the home up and running until his mood swings subside. I hope that's okay with you guys."

"It's fine, Claire. It's going to take months before that happens. Probably won't happen until after the wedding, I can guarantee you that."

Claire released a sigh of relief. "That's good to know. It gives the old Travis time to come back, who I really miss.

CHAPTER 12

Claire's words stuck with me for the rest of the day. *She misses the old Travis.* Other than his frequent outbursts of frustration, I hadn't noticed much difference. He was slowly gaining back weight and speaking much better. But My heart ached for Claire and what she must be going through. She is with him twenty-four-seven and sees it all. She doesn't talk to us about it or ask for our help. And now she is taking on the foster home and helping with the planning of our triple wedding. I don't know how she does it. I'm going to talk with Slater tonight and ask him not to pressure Claire and let her work at her own pace. I'll remind him, too, that she has to teach Travis a lot of things on the computer, which will take some time.

My first visit with the obstetrician did not go as planned. After going through a morning of having endless tests to check my health and a pregnancy test by the nurse to confirm my pregnancy, which came back positive, they wanted to do a prenatal ultrasound to have an estimated due date.

"Will we be able to see the baby?" Slater had asked as we followed the nurse to the room where the procedure would be done.

The nurse chuckled. "We may hear a very faint heartbeat, but it might be a little too early for that."

A half-hour later, I lay on a bed with my belly exposed and chilled by the gel on my stomach and the air conditioning of the room. Slater held my hand as we listened to the doctor evaluate her findings on the screen, and then suddenly Slater's hand had fallen away from mine. The news shocked him as much as it did me.

"Are you sure?" I asked, stunned by what I had just heard.

Doctor Louise nodded. "Oh, I'm quite sure. You are having twins."

I was numb and shared my shock with the nurse. "I can't believe we are having twins. It never crossed my mind that it could be a possibility because twins don't run in my family."

"Doesn't matter. Embryos can split at any time." She smiled. "I can see you are both surprised by the news. I'm going to leave you alone and let it sink in. Get dressed, and I'll come back to reschedule your next appointment."

After Doctor Louise had left, I turned to Slater. "Can you believe this? We are having twins."

Slater took my hand and smiled. Tears pooled in his eyes. For a guy, he never held back when it came to showing emotions. "I'm in shock." And then he cracked a laugh and stood. I watched and giggled as he paced the room, raking his hands through his hair. "Two babies at once." He stopped and grinned. "Are we ready for this?"

I laughed. "We will be by mid-June, I hope. Which is the estimated due date she gave us."

I flopped my head back and laughed. "Man, my mom was elated with one grandbaby. Wait till I tell her there are two."

"Do you want to call her now?"

I shook my head. "No, I'll wait until Friday when we are all meeting at Claire's house to discuss the wedding. I can tell everyone then." I pointed my finger at Slater and shook it. "Which means you can't go rambling to Ricky at work tomorrow. He told Jill right away after you had told him I was pregnant." I folded my arms and gave him a canning smile. "Jill can tell him when she goes home," I snickered. "She will love hearing the news first before Ricky."

Slater raised his hands. "Okay, I promise I won't tell. But it's not going to be easy." He curled his lip. "Is there anyone I can tell?"

I shook my head and laughed. "Nope, and I'm not going to either. It's only a few days. Oh, I can't wait to see their faces."

Slater approached me and leaned in. I melted when his warm lips touched mine. It was a loving, sensual kiss that lasted a good minute. "Sabela, each day keeps getting better and better with you. Do you mind If I come to Claire's with you? I want to be there when you tell them."

"I would love that. You can come later if you want to. When we are done talking about weddings, you might as well bring Ricky too."

Slater rubbed his hands together. "Oh, this is going to be a night to remember."

CHAPTER 13

We decided that Slater and Ricky would shoot some pool until I texted him to come over to Claire's.

We were all sitting around the table at Claire's house waiting for Jill, who hadn't shown up yet. Scottie brought his bag of chosen toys and was constantly playing on the living room floor, engrossed in his imaginary world.

"Has anyone heard from her?" I asked before taking a sip of my sparkling water. Now that I am responsible for two babies, no more beer for me. It still shocked me every time I thought of it. Slater is just as stunned as I am. I can see the joy in his eyes whenever we talk about it, but his voice doesn't hide his anxieties.

"How are we going to take care of two babies? We will never sleep," he said.

I agreed with a loud laugh. "I wonder if we'll have two girls, or two boys or even one of each."

"As long as only two come out and there isn't another one hiding somewhere. I don't think I can handle any more surprises," he joked.

I returned my focus to everyone sitting at the table. Mom sat next to me and asked me straight away how I was feeling. I put her at ease immediately and told her I was doing great. It seemed no one had heard from Jill. I checked the time on my phone and saw she was fifteen minutes late. "Should we get started without her?" I asked the group.

After the last nod, Claire came in from outside, where Travis and Tilly sat. There was a ring from the main entrance.

"That must be her," Claire announced before rushing to the intercom and confirming it after releasing the talk button. "She will be here in a few minutes." Claire unlocked the front door and left it open a crack for Jill before taking her seat at the table.

I glanced out at the deck. "Travis looks good, and he seems more alert," I told Claire.

Claire turned her head in his direction and released a caring smile. "He is. I think being involved in fostering homework is helping, and it's giving him a purpose. He still gets a little frustrated when he gets tired because he wants to keep working."

"What about his mood swings?" I asked, uncertain if I should have asked.

"He still has them. The seizure meds cause them. But since he's been helping me, they are not as frequent."

I smiled. "Oh, that is good news."

A few minutes later, we could hear footsteps racing down the hallway, and then Jill appeared after pushing open the door. "Hey, everyone," she said, catching her breath and pulling off her black leather jacket. "Sorry, I'm late. Work was a bitch today. I thought I would never get out of there."

Claire handed Jill a beer as she took a seat at the table. "Did he find someone to replace me?" Claire asked.

Jill nodded while gulping down her beer. She smacked her lips. "Yeah, a guy that's fresh out of college. He seems nice."

"Oh, good," Claire replied.

"Is Ricky still meeting Slater for a game of pool?" I asked Jill.

Jill didn't let her sarcasm go unnoticed when she replied. "Only if he can pull Ricky away from his video games. He got home early. Slater had an inspection on the site.

"You don't sound too happy, Jill," Claire stated.

Jill took another sip of beer and leaned back in her chair. "I shouldn't complain. I love everything about him, but man, he can play those games for hours. As soon as he comes home, he has a damn remote in his hand."

"I guess this was something you didn't know about him. Does it bug you that he is not giving you attention? Is that why it upsets you?" Claire asked.

Jill squirmed in her seat. "I guess. I know that's selfish of me, but I had no idea he spent so much time playing games. I swear he is addicted."

"Have you talked to him?" I asked.

Jill shook her head. "No, we are getting along so well. I'm still getting to know him, and I don't want to go back to my old ways when I complained about everything. I may scare him off," she laughed. "I tell myself that he is a few years younger than me, and men mature slower than women."

Everyone at the table laughed and nodded. "You got a point there, Jill. We all have our flaws." I told her and took another sip of water.

Jill's eyes narrowed. "Really, what flaws does Slater have? He seems so perfect."

I held my bottle of water while I spoke. "Well, he can't cook for one. He can't even cook an egg without burning it. Everything he cooks is well done—even pasta. So I do most of the cooking."

My mom's eyes showed her surprise. "Really, you never told me that."

"You've had his cooking, mom. Remember the hamburgers he barbecued at our house on July 4th?. They were like rubber."

"Oh, you are right. I had forgotten about those. You are right; he can't cook."

"What else?" Jill said as she rested her folded arms on the table.

I pondered for a minute. "Lately, he's been snoring, and it's loud," I giggled.

Claire matched my laugh. "I can't imagine him snoring."

"Oh, it keeps me awake. For the first time last week, I slept on the couch, but I just couldn't sleep. He was snoring so loud. I swear the room was shaking."

I smiled at Jill. "See, not everyone is perfect. Let Ricky play his games. It's probably his way of unwinding. I know Slater works him hard." I had an idea. "Hey, why not play with him?"

Jill shook her head. "Oh, hell no, he's killing a bunch of people, and there are lots of guns and shootings. Maggie gets lots of play-time with me when Ricky plays his games."

"Well, there you go. Maggie likes it when Ricky plays games," I joked. I looked down at my notes in front of me. "Okay then, let's talk about the wedding," I glanced over at Claire. "Claire, you had said you like the Fisherman's Grill for the reception."

"I do. I even took my mom and dad there yesterday, and they agreed. It's perfect and so close to the point. They have a huge banquet room in the back."

Abigail smiled. "It is beautiful. And they have a great menu."

I glanced over at Jill. "You liked it too, right?"

"Yep, they even have pink napkins and tablecloths."

I leaned back in my chair and rolled my eyes. "Jill, we've already said we are not having a pink wedding."

"This isn't the wedding, Sabela. It's the reception," Jill said with her lip curled.

"It's still part of the wedding, and I won't have pink at my wedding." I immediately regretted the last part of what I said and that I had practically yelled at Jill. It was her wedding too, and she reminded me.

"Sabela, it's my wedding too, and I want pink," she insisted.

"And I don't want pink either," Claire called out. "God, Jill, we've already been through this. It's two against one. I'm afraid we outvoted you."

My mom raised her hands. "Now, hold on a minute, ladies. Jill is right, it's her wedding too."

It shocked me that my mom was taking Jill's side and creased my brow. "Mom, what are you doing?"

"Let me talk, Sabela. I have an idea that might please all of you."

Jill clapped her hands. "Oh, goody, do I get my pink?"

My mom, who sat next to Jill, took her hand. "I don't see why not?"

"Mom," I moaned.

"Hear me out, Sabela. Now the way I see it is that the three of you are getting married on the beach, but each ceremony will be separate. The priest will ask each couple to announce their vows before going to the next couple. Is that correct?"

"Yes, that's right, mom. Your priest from your church, I hope. We all take turns getting married by the same priest. Our husbands will place the rings on our fingers, and then he will do the same with the next couple and then the third and then when he says you may kiss the bride. We all kiss our husbands at the same time."

"Will you be having bridesmaids?" Mom asked.

Jill quickly raised her hand. "I want Sadie to be mine."

My mom continued to talk. "Okay, well then, Jill should wear her pink at her wedding. That doesn't mean you and Claire have to wear pink. That is her part of the triple wedding and doesn't affect either of you. Why shouldn't she be allowed to wear a pink dress? And if Claire wants blue, yellow or whatever color she chooses, she should wear it. And the same goes for you, Sabela. Each girl should be able to pick their own colors for the actual ceremony, and then you can come together for a color scheme for the reception and whatever else you will be sharing."

I gave my mom a huge grin. I had a feeling she would have a solution. "I like that. What do you think, Claire?"

"I think it's brilliant. Jill gets her pink wedding dress and flowers, and we get to choose ours. I'm going to have the traditional white. What about you, Sabela?"

"It will be white for me too." I looked over at my mom. "Thanks, mom, you just saved the day."

With Jill content about her wedding dress, more brilliant ideas emerged from my mom's original one. Claire's mom, Abigail, suggested sending wedding invites based on our personal taste. Jill could send her pink ones out to her friends and family, and Claire and I could design our own and send them to our friends and family. My mom came up with another great idea for the cake. "Have a three-tier cake and three colors of icing if you need to," she suggested.

"What? A multi-colored cake?" I questioned.

"Why not? Jill's tier could be pink," mom said.

"I like it. It will be a one-of-a-kind cake." Claire said with a smile. "My tier could be light blue—like a pastel."

The idea was growing on me, and it made sense. "Okay then, my tier will be yellow."

"What a pretty cake that will be," my mom said with a large smile.

"Now we have to find a baker who will bake such a cake," I mentioned. I smiled at my mom. "Seeing how it was your idea, mom, do you want to go with me and check out some bakeries?"

"I would love to."

"And my parents can help me find printers for the invites, and Jill and I can look into florists," Claire said. Claire smiled at her parents across the table. "Do you want to do it this weekend, mom?"

Abigail gave a weak smile. "Oh, your father and I are going away this weekend. Can we do it when we get back?"

Claire creased her brow. "Going away, where are you going?"

I couldn't help noticing how Abigail stalled briefly and gave Claire's dad a subtle look. "We just feel like getting away and thought it would be nice to spend a weekend at a bed-and-breakfast. Your father needs the rest."

Claire shrugged her shoulders. "Okay, call me when you get

back." Claire suddenly sat up with bright eyes and changed the subject. "Wait, I've changed my mind on my dress."

I gave her a puzzled look. "You have?"

"Yes, I want it to match my tier on the cake. I'm going to wear a traditional wedding dress but have it dyed pastel blue." She paused. "And the flowers will be blue also."

I smiled and pondered the thought. "I like that. I'll do the same but in yellow."

Claire couldn't hide her excitement when she spoke again. "I have another idea."

"What's that?" I asked as I tried to keep up with writing all the great ideas in my notebook.

"Seeing how we are going with our color choices for the invites, flowers, cake, and dresses, why not do the same for the tablecloths at the reception?"

Jill replied, "What do you mean?"

"Well, for Jill's guests, she could have pink tablecloths and napkins. For mine pastel blue and for Sabela's, yellow."

Charlotte clapped her hands. "Oh, I love that. This just keeps getting better and better."

"I love it too," I squealed as I quickly added more notes.

My mom beamed a big smile while I texted Ricky and Slater. I was ready for them to come over.

"Oh, this is going to be such a wonderful wedding and so colorful," mom laughed.

CHAPTER 14

Slater and Ricky arrived within thirty minutes of texting. An excited Scottie greeted them when they walked through the door. "Daddy!" Scottie yelled as he jumped to his feet and raced into Slater's arms.

I pictured three kids racing into his arms and released a subtle smile. My heart was full from the thought.

"Hey, buddy," Slater said as he patted the top of Scottie's head.

Jill looked up, looking surprised as Ricky walked toward her and gave her a peck on the cheek. "What are you guys doing here? I thought you didn't want to help plan the wedding?"

"We don't," Ricky quickly replied, while glancing at Slater. "He said we gotta come here. I hope that is not why? But here I am. He's my boss." He chuckled. "I do what he says."

Claire stood. "Do you guys want a beer?"

"Sure," Slater and Ricky echoed.

"I texted Slater and asked them to come here," I announced. "Slater and I wanted to share some news with you."

The room fell silent. The only sound heard was Claire grabbing two beer bottles from the fridge.

"Is everything okay?' Ricky asked as he stood behind Jill and rubbed her neck.

Slater walked across the room and took Scottie's hand. "Come join us at the table, buddy. You may want to hear this too."

Scottie looked up at his dad. "Can I bring my car?"

Slater laughed. "Yes, you can bring your car."

Slater took a seat next to me and held my hand. Scottie sat in his lap. Butterflies danced in my stomach as we waited for Claire to return to the table.

My mom couldn't hide her concern. 'What's going on, Sabela?"

I gave her a caring smile. "Everything is fine, mom. I think you will like what we are about to tell you."

Claire rushed in. "Sorry, guys, I couldn't find the bottle opener." She glanced out on the deck and saw Travis was awake. Slater saw it too.

"Hey, Claire, can we open the sliding glass door so Travis can hear what we have to say. I don't want to leave him out."

"Wow, this must be something really big," Claire said as she walked over to the patio door and slid it open. Tilly immediately jumped from Travis's lap and danced around Claire's feet. Travis turned his head and smiled at her.

"Hey honey, Slater and Sabela have some news they are going to tell us, and they wanted to make sure you heard it too." She leaned over and kissed him on the lips. "How are you doing? Do you need anything?"

"I'm doing great. Had a good nap." He turned to look at Slater and waved. "I'm all ears, bro."

Slater smiled at me. "Do you want me to tell them, or you?"

I giggled. "You go ahead."

"Will one of you just tell us? The anticipation is killing me," Ricky hollered.

Slater raised his hands and smiled at me before he spoke. Scottie wiggled on his lap. "Listen to what I'm about to say, buddy." He whispered to his son. He cleared his throat, and the room fell silent. "As you all know, Sabela is pregnant, and we couldn't be happier. We found out that her due date is mid-June, which is plenty of time before our weddings, but..." he paused, smiling at me again.

I giggled, knowing what was coming next. "Tell them," I laughed louder.

"But we also found out at Sabela's first appointment that we are having twins."

Jill was the first to react with a scream. "What! Oh my god! I'm going to be an auntie to two babies. This is so frigging awesome."

My mom echoed her screams of joy as she left her seat and raced around the table to embrace Slater and me. "Oh my goodness, you are having twins! I'm going to have two grandbabies?"

"Yes, mom, we are having twins. Isn't it amazing?"

Tears of joy pooled in my eyes as the table exploded with cries of shock and congratulations. Slater hugged me and asked Scottie if he understood what he had just said.

"Sabbie is going to have two babies. Isn't that cool? You will be the big brother of two babies."

Scottie beamed him a smile. "That is cool. Can I get down now?"

After Scottie returned to his toys, Slater left the table and went outside to join Travis. I watched as the two men shook hands, and I couldn't help noticing how proud Slater looked.

Claire walked over to me, leaned down, and hugged me. "I'm so happy for you guys. This is the best news ever. If you need anything or if there is anything I can do for you, let me know."

"Claire, thank you. But you have your hands full with Travis."

"By the time these two babies of yours pop out, Travis should be doing much better. I don't plan on babysitting him for the rest of his life," she chuckled. "But these two babies of yours and Scottie, I'll watch any time."

I leaned in and hugged her. "I love you, Claire."

"I love you too. Hey, do you know if the twins will be boys or girls yet?"

I shook my head. "No, it's too early. My next appointment is in six weeks, and they said they would be able to tell by then. But we may not even ask. A surprise would be nice. We may even have one of each."

Claire's eyes lit up. "Oh, that would be cool. I never thought of that." She looked over at Scottie, who was now playing with Tilly. "I see he is all excited about the news."

I laughed and rolled my eyes. "I don't think he quite understands. He will soon learn when I give birth to these two."

We both looked across the table at Ricky and Jill making out at the table. Ricky was kissing Jill hard as he pulled back her hair and stroked her cheeks. "Hey guys, get a room. There is a child present," Claire hollered.

Ricky and Jill quickly broke apart. Jill snuggled against his chest as she giggled with her hands up to her mouth.

"Sorry, I haven't seen her all day. I lose all self-control when I am around her." He pulled Jill in and gave her a hard squeeze.

"Keep it up, and you'll be making babies next," Claire joked.

Jill quickly spoke. "Oh no, I'm on the pill. So there will be no kids for us just yet."

Ricky gave her a huge smile. "I like that. Which means someday."

Jill slapped his chest, "Ricky! Not so fast, we are not even married yet."

He gave her a sweet peck on the cheek. "But when we are, watch out."

Claire and I gave each other a stare. I had a feeling we were thinking the same thoughts. "Jill becoming a mom, wow."

CHAPTER 15

"What a brilliant idea my mom had for the wedding to incorporate all of our colors." I told Slater once we were home and in our bed. My head rested on his chest, and his arm cradled me.

Slater kissed the top of my head. "I think it's fantastic."

I breathed in his scent and kissed his bare chest with delicate kisses. "I love you so much, Slater." I continued to kiss his skin as I felt his body relax, and with one swift movement, he peeled back the covers away from our naked bodies. "I love you too, Sabela," he whispered as he stroked my back and pulled me in closer. "God, your skin is so soft."

"I love the way you taste," I said with my eyes closed as I traced his skin with my tongue down to his now erect manhood and took him in my mouth.

Slater released a loud moan, "Oh, hell yes."

Slater kneaded my buttocks as I continued to go down on him. I took in every inch, teasing him with my tongue. "You taste so damn good," I said, pulling away after a few minutes. "I want to feel you inside of me." I didn't wait for an answer and pulled my body on top of his. Slater immediately began caressing my breasts as I slowly lowered myself down to his prominent hard-on and rocked slowly. Slater arched his back and gave his hip a gentle thrust until he was all the way in.

"Oh yes," he moaned.

I leaned forward and kissed him passionately on the lips as we rocked together. Slater's hands moved to my hips, and our rhythm increased until I rode him with force. Our moans became louder and our breathing heavier. He massaged my skin deeper and with longer strokes as I continued to ride him. Feeling the orgasm approaching, I kissed Slater hard to muffle my sounds. Slater met me at the peak, and together we came, holding each other tight, our lips locked as our bodies jolted from the electrifying orgasm. It was pure bliss, and I collapsed into his arms, my body still trembling from the intense orgasm.

We must have fallen asleep straight away because I woke the following day cradled in Slater's arms with no sheets. Panic shot through me, and I sat up. Had I slept in? Was Scottie late for school? Suddenly I realized it was Saturday and, with a heavy sigh of relief, allowed my head to fall back into the pillow.

Later that morning, after my second cup of coffee and a morning spent playing Go Fish with Scottie and Slater, my mom called.

"Hey, mom, what's up?"

My mom sounded excited. "I think I have found a bakery for the cake. I've been making some calls, and this guy loves the idea we have for the cake, and his prices are really good. He says if we want to, we can go by his store this afternoon and discuss it."

"Great! Let's do it. Slater is off today. He can watch Scottie. Give me the address, and I will meet you over there. Will two o'clock work?"

"That will be perfect." My mom replied before reeling off the address.

When I walked into Bianchi's Italian Bakery a few hours later with my mom, I thought I had died and gone to heaven. The sweet smell of fresh baked goods and roasted coffee overpowered me. The strong sweet aromas of cakes and pastries baking in the oven took me back to my childhood days, when my mom baked on weekends.

I scanned the large store with wall-to-wall glass cases filled with delicious homemade Italian cookies, pastries, and cakes. From all the biscotti and croissants to Mezzaluna cookies, Brutti Ma Buoni cookies, Cannelloni and Torcetti, I inhaled deeply and suddenly had a sweet tooth. "My god, mom, this place is amazing. How come I've never heard of it? It's only thirty minutes away."

An elderly cheerful lady wearing a black dress and white apron greeted us with a friendly smile and spoke with a thick Italian accent. "Ciao, welcome to Bianchi's Bakery. How can I help you?"

My mom approached the counter. "Hello, what a beautiful place you have here."

The lady smiled and gave us a slight no, "Grazie, my friend."

"I spoke to Mr. Lorenzo this morning about a wedding cake for my daughter. He told me we could come by this afternoon."

The lady raised her hands and gave us a greater smile. "That is my son. I will fetch him for you. Uno momento," she said as she hurried off and disappeared behind a set of two swinging doors.

A few minutes later, a handsome, dark-haired, middle-aged man appeared and walked around the counter to join us. He smiled and took my hand and gave it a gentle kiss. "Signora, it's a pleasure to meet you. I am Lorenzo Bianchi"

His friendly introduction touched me, and I gave him a warm smile. "It's a pleasure to meet you too." I patted my mom's shoulder. "This is my mom, Charlotte. She is the woman you spoke to this morning on the phone."

Lorenzo turned to face my mom, took her hand, and gave it a soft kiss. I giggled as I watched my mom blush.

"A beautiful lady," Lorenzo said with a luring smile, followed by a wink. He raised his hands and spun around. "Please let me show you our bakery. It has been in my family for three generations."

After an amazing tour and some fantastic roasted fresh coffee and chocolate-dipped biscotti, my mom and I were sold and eagerly told Lorenzo our plans for the cake. He loved it and added some ideas of his own. He would make an almond icing. Drizzle chocolate over the cake and add fresh fruit, including grapes, kiwi, raspberries, strawberries, and blackberries. I smiled as he took my mom's hand again, kissed it, and gave her his card. "I will call you soon my beautiful lady with details and a time for you to come in and try some samples."

My mom cupped his card in her hand and smiled. "Thank you so much. I look forward to it."

When we were free of the store and standing outside on the busy street, I turned and faced my mom. "Was he flirting with you?" I said with a playful grin.

My mom waved her hands in front of my face. "What? Are you crazy? Lorenzo was just being a nice businessman. He wasn't flirting with me." She shook her head in an attempt to discard my notion. "And besides, Italians are known to be extra friendly."

I folded my arms and laughed at my mom's feeble excuse. "Oh, come on, mom, he was definitely flirting with you. It's my wedding, and he spent more time talking to you about the cake."

My mom raised her brow. "No, he did not. You're imagining things, Sabela."

I laughed again. "No, I'm not, mom. Oh and another thing, he only kissed my hand once. How many times did he kiss yours? He was definitely flirting with you. And who got his business card, I might add."

My mom reached into her pocket and pulled out Lorenzo's card. She looked down at it as she spoke, whispering, "Do you really think he was flirting with me?" She looked up. Her eyes were sad. "But I'm a widow, Sabela."

I rested my hand on her shoulder and gave it a gentle squeeze.

"Mom, it doesn't mean you have to stop living. I know how much you loved and still do love dad. But he would never want you to stop living your life. Dad will always be a part of you, but you have a huge heart, and I know you have room to let others in."

Tears pooled in my mom's eyes, and I held out my arms.

"I miss your father so much."

"Aww, mom, I know you do. I miss him too. Be happy for dad. Live your life the way you want to, and always carry dad in your heart."

With a subtle movement of her hand, my mom returned Lorenzo's card to her pocket. "I will. Your dad would have been so proud of you."

"Thank you, mom. Hey, do you want to grab some coffee and share fond memories of dad?" I asked as I locked my arm with hers.

She smiled, "I would like that."

CHAPTER 16

*A*fter my mom's brilliant idea about incorporating all of our color choices into the wedding, the plans seemed to go much more smoothly. We were all working well together as a team, and things were falling into place.

Three months after announcing we were having twins, we had booked the reception at the Fisherman's Grill; I had ordered flowers in all three colors along with our bouquets. Invitations would arrive in the next few weeks, ready to be mailed out, and Lorenzo would be making the cake. Ricky had some friends that played in a band, and we all loved the sound samples and made the unanimous decision to have them play at the reception. We all agreed to have only the sound of the ocean at the wedding ceremony on the beach.

Today we are shopping for wedding dresses. It will be a full-day event with Sadie tagging along to help Jill choose her dress. My mom will join us, along with Claire's mom, Abigail. Sadie was the one who found the store, and when they told her they could also dye the dresses, we were excited to check it out.

I stood in front of the full-length mirror, wearing a white floral summer dress and white sandals. Slater stood behind me with his head resting on my shoulder and his arms wrapped around my waist. My pregnancy was now showing. He rubbed my belly as he gazed at me through our reflection in the mirror.

"Are you sure you don't want me to come with you?"

I nuzzled my head against his. "No, it's bad luck for the groom to see the dress. And besides, you have to watch Scottie."

"I have a question," he asked, rubbing my belly again.

"What's that?"

"Well, if you buy the dress today, won't it be too big by the time we get married? You will have had the twins by then."

I turned to face him and placed my hands on his chest. "I'm going to ask them about having it altered after the twins are born. I'm sure they can do that."

"Oh, that's a good idea. I never thought of that. So when will I see you?"

I looked in the mirror and teased my hair, "probably not until tonight. Three women buying three wedding dresses in one day will take some time. We all made a commitment that we were not leaving the store until we had all our dresses picked out. This is the day. The only day we have put aside to do this."

Slater chuckled. "Talk about pressure. I think I'd rather stay home."

I laughed, "Smart decision." I scanned the bedroom. "Now, where did I put my purse? Jill and Claire will be here any minute in Jill's car."

Slater looked surprised. "You're going in Jill's car?"

"Yeah, her pink Mustang is a fun car to ride in. I've not ridden in it in a while, and this is a big day. It will be fun, and besides, Jill insisted. She wants to show the store the color of her car so they can match it with her dress. She wants her dress to be the same color." I snickered and rolled my eyes.

"Ha! That's a first. A bride wants her wedding dress to match her car," Slater laughed. "Maybe Scottie and I will go by and hang out with Travis for a while. Will he be home?"

I spotted my purse on the bed and grabbed it. "Yes, Claire's dad is going to be there too for a while. Travis is doing much better. He's been driving short trips with Claire and doing really good. Claire is not ready to let him drive alone yet, even though Travis is more than ready," I laughed. "Claire said in a few months when he is off his meds; she would feel more comfortable. But she has been leaving him alone at the condo now and then for a while so she can take care of some things. She makes sure he has plenty of work to do and leaves him a list of stuff to do for the foster home." I smiled. "They both seem a lot happier, and I can see the excitement in their eyes when we have our meetings about the foster home and discuss the progress we are making."

Slater matched my smile, "me too. Travis has come a long way. I'm so glad we did this and have them be in charge of the home."

"It was all your idea, Slater. I just saw what a brilliant one it was and agreed. What you are doing is amazing. Not only will you be bringing children into Travis and Claire's lives and allowing them to be parents, but you are also bringing a sense of belonging and love to some lucky foster kids. It's a beautiful thing."

"It's what they were meant to do."

"You're right. I can't wait until we are official and can start helping some kids."

"Well, they have approved the permits. Claire is taking all the necessary classes, and Travis is taking some too. We have a meeting next week with our attorney to discuss the legal side of the business and to begin the process of also being an adoption agency which both Travis and Claire said they wanted to do."

"How much longer do you think it will be?"

"I'm not sure. Our attorney will be able to answer that," he smiled. "Maybe it will be their wedding gift."

I gave him a huge grin. "That would be amazing."

A car horn interrupted our conversation. "That must be Jill. Wish me luck. I'm going to need it."

He threw me a sexy smile, making it hard to leave. "Good luck, I don't envy you."

I gave him a playful slap on his chest. "Well, it will be your turn soon."

"What does that mean?"

"Well, you, Travis, and Ricky will have to go shopping for your suits soon."

Slater creased his brow. "We do?"

"Well, of course, unless you were planning on getting married in shorts."

"Can we?" he joked.

I slapped him again, "Slater!"

Jill blasted on her horn again. I gave Slater a smooch on the lips. "It's time to go. I'll see you tonight." I then raced down the stairs and out the door.

CHAPTER 17

The loud music blaring from Jill's car hit me as soon as I stepped outside. I soon sang along to the lyrics of "Like A Virgin" by Madonna as I stepped into the front passenger seat and hugged Jill. I turned to face Claire, who was sitting in the back, swaying to the beat of the music. "Hey, Claire," I said as Jill pulled out of the driveway.

Jill reached over and rubbed my belly. "Look at you. You are beginning to show. I wonder how big you are going to get with two babies."

I laughed as I shadowed Jill's rubs. "Not too big, I hope. How much more can one's stomach grow in five and half months?" I said in a louder voice than normal, trying to be heard over Madonna.

"When do you go back to the doctors?" Claire hollered from the back seat. Also, trying to be heard over the music.

"In about three weeks, in January. I wanted to get Christmas out of the way." I turned and looked at Jill. "Can you turn down the music so we can hear each other talk?"

Jill granted my request but continued to move to the beat. "Can you believe Christmas is only nine days away? I bet Scottie is excited."

"He is. We put the tree up last week. Hey, are you guys still coming over for dinner at four? My mom will be there." I turned my head again and spoke to Claire. "Your parents are invited too."

"Yes, we will be there. My mom and dad are looking forward to it. It's been a while since we spent a Christmas together."

I looked over at Jill. "How about you and Ricky? Are you coming?"

"Oh, I'd love to, but we are going to Vegas with Logan and Sadie." Jill wore a look of guilt. "I hope you don't mind. I just need to get away and let loose," she laughed.

"You know I've never met them," I announced.

Jill's jaw dropped. "You haven't?" I thought you had. How have you not met them?"

"Nope, I haven't. I know she worked with you and used to be your roommate. You talk about her and Logan all the time. Didn't they elope to Vegas?"

Jill cracked a loud laugh. "Yes, they did, and they are doing great—married life suits them. Well, shoot, I'm sorry, I thought you had met them. I know Claire has. Sadie started working with us before Claire quit."

"I met her, but that was before we were friends, Jill," Claire said. "Sadie and I didn't talk much when I worked there."

Jill reached over and pushed buttons on the dash until a Beyonce song played. "Sadie is meeting us at the bridal dress boutique." She turned and smiled. "You will finally get to meet her."

"Great! I'm looking forward to it." I leaned back in my chair. Jill had the top down in the car, and the wind racing over my face and through my hair was exhilarating. "So, how far is this place?" I asked with my eyes closed.

"About forty minutes," Jill replied. She then leaned over and nudged my knee. "Hey, can you believe we are all getting married and settling down?"

It was impossible to sit back and relax with Jill chatting away. I pulled myself up from my relaxed position and smiled at her. "I love that we are sharing our wedding day together. I think it's pretty special."

"It is," Claire said from the back seat. "It was a brilliant idea you had, Sabela."

This time, Jill nudged my arm. "Hey, are we going to have a bachelorette party? We could go to a strip club and get wasted."

"Jill, I'm three and a half months pregnant. I can't get wasted, and I sure as hell don't want to have some oiled-up male dancer groveling all over me in my condition, especially sober," I laughed.

Jill's smile turned to a frown. "Aww, party pooper."

Claire sided with me. "Come on, Jill, don't give Sabela a hard time. Put yourself in her shoes. By the time we get around to having some kind of party, Sabela might be six months pregnant. That won't be any fun for her, and like she said, she can't drink either."

I patted Jill's knee. "We will think of something, I promise. Maybe we can do something with the guys. Have a party together instead of apart. I've never understood that, anyway. I want to party with the man I'm going to be with for the rest of my life, not some stranger."

"I never understood it either," Claire said. "Partying with the guys is not a bad idea. What do you think, Jill?"

Jill didn't sound too convinced. "Oh, I don't know. It just seems weird. I've been to many bachelorette parties, and the grooms were never there." She turned and looked at both of us. "It's supposed to be a girls' night out—drinks, sexy men dancing. One last hurrah before we tie the knot."

I felt guilty listening to Jill, who didn't hide her disappointment. I knew in a few months I wouldn't be up to partying like she had in mind. Even now, as I rubbed my stomach, the idea didn't appeal to me. Then it occurred to me. Slater and I hadn't even discussed whether he would have a bachelor party with the guys. "Hey, has Travis or Ricky mentioned a bachelor party to either of you?"

Claire and Jill both shook their heads at the same time. Claire spoke. "Well, Travis can't, that's for sure. He's still recovering. No alcohol for him."

"Ricky hasn't said anything either," Jill said as she made a left turn.

"Don't you think we should discuss this with the guys?" I questioned. "Let's see what they say. Maybe celebrating together might be better with me pregnant and Travis still recovering from his accident."

Finally, Jill agreed. "Yeah, you are probably right. I wasn't thinking, sorry guys."

Jill turned right into a parking lot of the Bridal Affair store and turned the car off once she was in park. I scanned the area and saw the parking lot wasn't even a third occupied. "It's pretty quiet here."

"Yeah, Sadie said that it's a good time to shop for bride's dresses. Everyone is thinking about Christmas, not weddings."

I nodded. "That makes sense."

Jill's phone dinged, and she read the text message that had just come in. "It's Sadie. She will be here in about ten minutes. Let me text her back and tell her we will meet her inside."

Within thirty minutes of arriving, our party was complete. My mom had arrived, and so had Claire's mom. Sadie arrived last after getting stuck in traffic two blocks away from where a traffic light was out. She and Jill greeted each other with loud screams, causing me to look the other way as shoppers looked on. It was good to put a face to the name finally.

She approached me with her arms extended and wore a stunning smile. "You must be Sabela."

I smiled and met her in a friendly embrace. "I am. It's so good to meet you finally." I stepped back and admired her outfit consisting of a mini denim skirt, a flimsy yellow cotton tank top, and cute red cowboy boots. "Let me guess; you are a country girl."

Sadie laughed as she glanced down at her attire. "Now, whatever makes you say that?" She glanced over my shoulder at Claire, who was talking to her mom, and waved. "Hi, Claire."

Claire looked taken aback by her friendly greeting and waved back. "Hi, Sadie. Thanks for finding this place. It's awesome."

I didn't sense any tension between Sadie and Claire, which had been my concern, knowing Sadie was there for Jill when Travis had left her. I was relieved that everyone had moved on and no grudges were being held.

From where I stood in the enormous store with high ceilings, I suddenly felt overwhelmed by the vast amount of choices of dresses to choose from. The building was wall-to-wall dresses, bridesmaids' dresses, veils, and tuxedos. How was I ever going to decide in one day? My mom must have read my mind, who stood next to me wearing the same worried look. "There are so many to choose from, Sabela. Where do we start?"

I spotted a young blonde walking towards us with a friendly smile. She wore a name tag on her white shirt. "With that lady coming our way," I replied.

I heard giggles coming from behind us and turned my head. It did not surprise me to see it was Jill and Sadie. Jill had a short mini dress held up to her body as Sadie laughed and pulled it away. I shook my head and giggled.

The young blonde approached us. She was definitely younger than my twenty-eight years by a few years, but she had class. Her blonde hair was tied back in a ponytail, and she wore very little makeup, but then again, she didn't need to. Her white cotton shirt was buttoned high, with a black-tie hanging loosely around her neck, and a mid-length black skirt completed her wardrobe. She extended her hand and spoke with a clear, affirmative voice. "Hello, ladies, do we have a bride-to-be amongst you?"

Claire, Jill and I giggled at the same time as we raised our hands and said, "Me."

I laughed again, and this time was the only one to speak. "We are all getting married on the same day. We are having a triple wedding."

"The blonde's eyes lit up. "Well, I am Lucy. I'd be happy to help you and what a great idea to get married on the same day."

"Well, if you work off commission, this should be a good day for you," Jill joked.

After filling Lucy in on our request and that we wanted the dresses dyed, she turned us onto a brilliant idea of dip-dyeing the dresses. "It's amazing, and the dresses look so beautiful. I can only imagine having three different colors at your wedding. It's going to look fantastic."

Claire still wasn't convinced. "So only the bottom of the dress is dyed?" she asked.

Lucy nodded. "That is correct, but the color gradually fades until above the waistline, where it is completely white." She motioned her hand for us to follow her. "Come with me. I will show you samples."

Lucy wasn't kidding. The three dresses on display were stunning. One was navy blue. Another was red, and the third was pink.

Claire's eyes turned wide. "Wow! I love these. How much does it cost?"

"It averages about $300 a dress to dip dye them plus the cost of the dress."

"And you can do this with any dress?" I asked.

"Yes, pretty much. And the veils too."

Claire looked at me and grinned. "That's not a bad price. Let's do this. It's much better than dying the whole dress."

"I agree." I turned to face Jill. "What do you think, Jill?"

"I love it. Can we do a pink one that matches my car?"

"I'm sure we can," Lucy said with a chuckle.

I don't know how many dresses we looked at or tried on, and I had no idea how many hours we were at the store, but it was definitely a fashion show to remember. Lucy's patience was incredible. She was definitely in the right line of work and had an honest opinion about the dresses we tried on. If she didn't like one, she didn't hesitate to let us know and tell us why. I was thankful for her honesty. Jill was the only one that got a little touchy when Lucy told her one of the dresses was a little too tight, and too much cleavage was showing. Lucy had suggested toning it down a bit.

"Yeah, Jill, you look like a bride stripper," Claire added.

Jill had narrowed her eyes at Claire and snarled. "No, I do not. I want to show off my body. If you have it, flaunt it. Isn't that what they say?"

Claire rolled her eyes and gave me a stare, searching for backup. I shifted in my seat and chose my words carefully. "Jill, we all know you have a great body. So does Ricky, and everything you wear shows that, but don't you think this is just a little too much for your wedding day. You are beautiful, Jill, and you have class, but to be honest, this dress looks cheap."

Claire gave me a satisfying nod. I was thankful when our moms agreed and voiced it.

Jill took one last look at the dress that we had all criticized and did a final twirl in front of the full-length mirror. "Yeah, I see it now. I keep looking down to make sure my boob hasn't popped out. It feels like it could at any moment. There's no support." She turned and giggled. "That would be awful if it happened at the wedding." She glanced at us through the reflection of the mirror. "Thanks, ladies. Okay, on to the next one."

Hours later, we had our dresses picked out. I had spent some time talking to Lucy about having my dress altered after the twins were born, and she said it wouldn't be a problem. Jill's dress would be dip-dyed to match her car, and even our moms said they would find a dress to match our chosen colors. Claire's mom would look for a pastel blue, and my mom would shop for a yellow one. Jill said she would mention it to her mom and ask that she wear a pink dress.

Our dresses were perfect for each of us and matched our personalities. I had chosen a long Bohemian mermaid dress with a lace train. The sleeves were short, and it had a v-neck and opened back. I knew as soon as I slipped it on that it was the one.

Claire's was more formal, but looked beautiful on her. It was an off-the-shoulder sleeveless lace dress with a beautiful flare to it below the waistline, and Jill looked stunning in the dress she finally decided on. It was a gorgeous, flirty, backless spaghetti lace dress that I could picture swaying in the gentle breeze at the beach.

Satisfied with our choices and happy parents, we all suddenly realized we hadn't eaten all day and felt our stomachs gurgling.

"Where should we eat?" Jill asked after we had thanked Lucy for everything and scheduled an appointment in six weeks to pick up the dresses after they had been dipped.

Claire was on the phone, checking on Travis.

"Everything okay?" I asked after she had hung up.

She nodded. "Yes, Slater and Scottie are with him."

"Oh, good. I'll call him on the way to the restaurant? Did we decide on a place yet?"

Claire's mom spoke. "There is a really nice restaurant not too far from here that has really good food and serves everything from steaks, seafood, and burgers. Jeffery and I often eat there."

"Sounds good to me." Jill quickly said, "I'm starving."

After finding the restaurant on my phone and getting the directions, Claire told her mom we would meet her over there, and I told my mom the same thing.

While driving to the restaurant, I finally had a sense of relief with choosing and buying our wedding dresses behind us. I had been dreading it for months and didn't know what to expect. I actually thought there would be more drama with three ladies buying dresses together, but everything went pretty well.

I have only known Claire for roughly half a year, but I couldn't help noticing that we shared a lot of similar tastes when it came to the wedding. Sometimes I felt like we were ganging up on Jill. I've known Jill much longer, almost five years, and never paid attention to how much different we really are. Yes, she loves pink and likes to be the center of attention, but I feel much older than her sometimes, even though we are the same age. Maybe I'm becoming more mature with this pregnancy. I've certainly toned down a lot. Jill and I have had some crazy times in the past. Partying and getting wasted some nights, but when she met Travis, that soon came to an end, and we saw more of each other only at work and when we shared our lunches together. Since she split with Travis, she seems younger again.

We were the last to arrive at the restaurant. We found our parents sipping on red wine. Claire's mom, Abigail, raised her hand high and waved, followed by a friendly smile. My mom was excited to recap the day over dinner, and it warmed my heart to see the excitement in her eyes. They were bright as she looked at me and patted her chest. "I can't believe my baby girl is getting married. Oh, how I wish your father could be with us."

"He is, mom. I feel him." I raised my glass, and the rest did the same. "To dad."

"To dad," my friends and mom echoed.

"I miss you, Dad," I whispered under my breath before taking a sip of my iced tea.

After placing our orders and insisting that lunch was on me, Claire silenced us with her words.

"I've been waiting until we were all together to tell you something and ask your advice."

The table immediately fell to a complete silence as all eyes focused on Claire. My first thought was Travis. Did she have some bad news? "Claire, what's going on? Is Travis okay?"

Claire gave me a caring smile. "Travis is fine. But this does have something to do with him."

"Go on, we're listening," I said, egging her on to continue.

Claire glanced over at Jill. "Well, when Travis was in a coma, Jill and I came across some old photos of Travis. We both knew that he was raised in foster homes and had never met his birth mother."

"That's true. And then, a few days later, I found his birth certificate." Jill added, beaming with pride.

Claire nodded. "You did. It was a huge piece of the puzzle. I intended to try and look for his parents. But with Travis's accident and his recovery, I knew I wouldn't have time, plus I wouldn't know where to begin."

Jill's eyes widened. "That right, and you said you had hired a company that looks for lost parents and other family members," Jill gasped. "Wait! Did they find them?"

Claire hesitated and then revealed a small smile. "They found one of them."

Jill raised her hands to her mouth to silence her scream. "Oh my god! That's amazing. When are you going to meet them? Does Travis know?"

Claire raised her hands and cut Jill off. "Hold on a second. I just found this out a few days ago. And now I find myself not knowing what to do."

"Well, who did they find? His mom or dad?" Claire's mom, Abigail, asked.

"They found his mom, Caroline Trent. She has no idea where the father is. The father's family moved away shortly after Caroline had given birth to Travis."

I nodded. "Oh, I see. Are they going to try and find the dad?"

"I don't think so. They have no leads. His name was Bobby Clay. That's all they could tell me."

My mom had a question. "If the father's last name is Clay, why is Travis's name Trent after his mother's?"

Jill raised her hand like she was on a quiz show. "I know. Claire and I researched this together. If the parents are not married and the father is not present, then the baby takes the mother's last name."

Claire nodded. "Jill is correct."

"So, what is the problem?" I asked. "You've found his mom. Which is what you hired this company to do." I paused. "Have you told Travis yet?"

Claire shifted in her seat. "No, I haven't."

Sadie joined in on the conversation. "Do you think he will be mad?"

"I don't think so. We had talked about it in the past. I had told Jill the same thing because she had asked me that too. He had no objections to me looking for his parents."

I was puzzled. "So why haven't you told him?"

"Well, I thought about inviting her to the wedding as a surprise guest for Travis."

Jill reacted first. "Oh wow, that is heavy."

I wasn't too sure about Claire's plan. It made me feel uneasy. "Oh, I don't know, Claire. Have you spoken to her at all? What does she sound like?"

"I haven't. I wanted to run it by you guys first and see what you think. I think it would be an amazing gift for Travis to have his birth mom at his wedding and meet her for the first time."

"Are you planning on meeting her first?" I asked, still unsure about her idea.

"I hadn't thought about it. I pictured us both meeting her for the first time together. It would feel wrong for me to meet her before Travis and not tell him about it. He should be the one to meet her first. Not me."

Claire's mom gave us her thoughts. "I see your point, Claire, but inviting someone to the wedding whom you have never met sounds risky to me. You know absolutely nothing about her."

Jill butted in. "I agree. She may be a raving lunatic."

I chuckled. "Jill has a point. I suggest talking to her on the phone. Get a feel for her and see how you guys hit it off before making any decisions."

Everyone at the table nodded in agreement, including Claire.

"I was planning on calling her tomorrow."

"Don't tell her about the wedding yet," my mom insisted.

"Why not?" Claire asked.

My mom rolled her eyes at Claire. "Because, more than likely, she'll be expecting an invitation. Get to know her a little. Make a few phone calls. See if you can be friends."

I looked over at my mom. "If it turns out they don't get along. Then what? Say nothing to Travis. Claire can't do that. Even if it turns out Claire doesn't get along with her, she has to tell Travis. She can't keep this from him."

"You are right, Sabela. I have no intentions of not telling him. I just would like to surprise him."

"Well, no matter how you tell him, it's going to be a surprise." I laughed.

Claire raised her hands in defeat. "Okay, you win. I will talk to her tomorrow and say nothing about the wedding. But if after a few phone calls we are hitting it off, I'll tell her."

I gave her a stare. "And then what?"

"And then I'll decide on whether to tell Travis or make it a surprise."

"How would you not be able to tell Travis? That's a huge secret. It would kill me." I told Claire.

"Oh, Claire is good at keeping secrets. She and Travis were dating for months before they told me." Jill narrowed her eyes on me. "And you knew it too. You both are good at keeping secrets. Claire would have no problem keeping this from Travis."

"Okay, enough, Jill. Why bring up the past. We have all moved on. I'll let you all know how my phone call goes tomorrow," Claire snapped.

Jill folded her arms. "Well, let me know first. I was with you when you started this thing."

"Fine, Jill. I will call you first." Claire turned her head and saw the waiter coming towards our table with plates of food. "Great, here is our food. Let's eat."

CHAPTER 19

I wasn't completely sold on Claire's idea and mentioned it to Slater when I got home. Scottie had just gotten out of the bath, and Slater was helping him get into his PJs.

"And she hasn't told Travis anything?" Slater asked while kneeling and holding out a pajama leg for Scottie.

"Nope. Travis has no idea. I didn't tell Claire this, but what if she keeps it from him until the wedding and Travis is mad? Maybe he wants to be prepared or warned first. Talk about being put on the spot." I sat down on the chair while Slater finished dressing Scottie. "I mean, if I did something like that to you, how would you react?"

"I honestly don't know. I think it's neat in a way, and it will be a pretty special moment for the two of them."

"But what if they don't hit it off? What if Travis has buried hidden resentments that come unleashed when he meets her?"

Slater laughed and watched as Scottie hurried off to the couch to watch TV. "What are you expecting to happen, Sabela? Some big standoff between them. Maybe you are overthinking this just a little."

I rolled my eyes. I wasn't getting through to him. "Aren't you a little worried that this may go wrong and could end up being a nightmare and ruin the whole wedding?"

Slater shrugged his shoulders. "No, I'm not. Sorry. I actually think it's pretty cool. The fact that they have found his mom is amazing, to begin with. To surprise him on their wedding day, I think, is a great idea."

I ran my hands through my hair and pulled it back away from my face. "I can't believe we disagree on this. I'm taken aback by your reaction. "

"Maybe it's because you are pregnant," he joked. "More stuff bothers you. You are much more sensitive and picky."

I creased my brow. "How?"

"Well, for starters, you used to walk around here barefoot all the time. Now you can't stand it and have to have socks or slippers on."

"My feet itch from the carpet and tickle on the tile."

"Yeah, but it only started bothering you since you've been pregnant. You used to love coffee. And you suddenly hate the smell of coffee and drink tea in the morning. I still love coffee, but you complain about the smell every time I make a pot."

"It makes me gag."

Slater laughed again. "It never used to. Anyway, my point is, things seem to bother you more. If Claire wants to surprise Travis, it's none of our business. We can only hope it's a success."

I knew I was beaten. I had no defense. "Fine. I'll stay out of the way."

After Scottie went to bed, Slater and I snuggled on the couch with my body laying flat and my head resting in his lap. His hand rested on my stomach, which he gently massaged. "Are they kicking yet?"

"No. The doctor said I could start feeling it any day now."

"I want my hand to be right here when they do," he said, giving my stomach a slight squeeze.

"Okay. I'll tell the twins not to kick until you are home." I patted his hand. "You know what else came up today?"

"No, what?"

"Bachelorette and bachelor parties. Jill wants to know if we are having one."

"What did you tell her?"

"Well, Claire and I kind of agreed on this. I'm pregnant and can't drink alcohol, and Travis is still recovering. I suggest partying together, us girls and you guys."

"Oh, I bet Jill was bummed."

"Yeah, she was. I think she wanted to go to a strip club."

"Well, if that's what she wants, she should go. Doesn't mean you and Claire should go? She has other friends, I'm sure that I can go with her."

"Yeah, there's Sadie. Jill gave me a weird stare when I suggested all of us get together. I got the feeling she wanted a traditional girls' night out with no guys. I don't think she was too keen on my idea."

"I kind of like it. The thought of you partying and pregnant doesn't sit too well with me."

"That's what I was trying to tell Jill." I gave him a flirty smile. "But I have some ideas that might change her mind."

Slater chuckled. "Oh really? And what might they be?"

I matched his laugh. "I'm not telling yet. It might be a surprise. I have to talk to Claire and Jill first."

I laid in his lap and giggled at the thoughts I was having, and wondered if my friends would go for it.

"So you are not going to tell me?" Slater persisted, while I continued to laugh.

I shook my head and gave him a big smile. "Nope. Now I'm not saying anymore. Let's cuddle and watch a movie."

∽

Up until now, even with twins, my pregnancy was going smoothly—no morning sickness or weird eating habits. No unusual pains and I still had the energy to go about my days. This was the first day I felt under the weather and decided just to take it easy and be a couch potato.

I had called Slater at work and told him I was putting off all my office duties until tomorrow. He wanted to come home and be with me, but I insisted he stay at work, and I would call him if I felt any worse. The only thing I asked was if he could pick up Scottie from school.

While lying on the couch feeling nauseated and experiencing the pains of a severe headache, my phone rang. I grabbed my phone and saw it was Claire, and then I suddenly remembered she was going to call Travis's mom today. I quickly answered the call.

"Hey, Claire."

"Hey."

Her tone sounded happy. "So, did you call Travis's mom?"

"I did, and I just got off the phone with Jill. Remember, she asked that I call her first. Anyway, I wanted to call you before she did. I'm sure she is dying to tell you."

I was anxious to hear how it went and sat up while trying to ignore my pounding headache. "So, how did it go?"

"It went okay. As soon as I told her who I was, she started crying hysterically. I felt really bad."

"Did she tell you anything about herself?"

"Yes, we were on the phone for over an hour."

I couldn't hide the excitement in my voice and wanted to hear everything. "So what did she tell you?. How does she sound?"

"The first thing she told me after she composed herself was that she never got over giving up Travis. It brought tears to my eyes. She told me that a day hadn't gone by where she hadn't thought about him. Wondering what he looked like, what he did for a living. She wondered if he had a family and kids."

I clutched my heart when I spoke. "Aww, that is so sad. I could never imagine the heartache of giving up a child."

"She also told me that Travis's birthdays are really bad for her. It brings back such heart-wrenching memories of when she handed him over and never saw him again."

"How come she never looked for him?"

"She was afraid of his reaction or being rejected by him. She never had the courage to do it."

"I can understand that. No wonder she bawled her eyes out."

"Yeah, it was a pretty emotional conversation. She had me crying a few times."

I wanted to know more. "So, is she married or has any kids?"

"No, she was never married and has no kids." Giving up Travis really messed with her life. The idea of having kids after giving one up seemed so wrong and unfair to Travis. She never had any interest in marriage and has been estranged from her parents since she left home at seventeen. She never forgave them for making her give him up."

"So where is she now? How old is she?" I had so many questions. "What does she do for a living?"

Claire laughed. "Hold on a second. Well, she is forty-five. She seems so young to be Travis's mom, but then again, she was fifteen when she had him. She lives in Seattle, Washington, by herself. She confided in me that she spent many years addicted to drugs and alcohol and has been sober for five years."

"Wow. I was stunned by what Claire had just revealed. She's had a rough life."

"Yeah, she said she was depressed for many years, all stemming from giving up Travis, which led to getting into alcohol and drugs for an escape. She is really proud of herself for getting clean and turning her life around. She went back to school and is now a nurse."

"That is fantastic."

"She sounded really nice on the phone. Jill insists we invite her to the wedding and not tell Travis. I'm not too sure. I felt guilty talking to her before Travis. Like I was betraying him."

"You are not betraying him. If it weren't for you, you would not have had that conversation with her today. I think what you did was beautiful. When you first told me, I wasn't sold on the idea of surprising Travis with her presence at the wedding, but after hearing from you today, I think it is a fabulous wedding gift for Travis."

Claire raised her voice a notch. "You do? So I should invite her to the wedding?"

"Sure. She probably has to arrange her time off work and accommodations here in San Diego. She will need plenty of notice to do that."

"You are right. I'm going to call her tomorrow."

"Now, the only thing you have to do is keep it a secret from Travis." I reminded her. "Do you think you will be able to do that?"

"It will be hard because I am dying to tell him, but I will do my best."

CHAPTER 20

*A*fter hanging up the phone, I remained on the couch, lost in my thoughts. Images of the colorful wedding we were putting together danced in my mind. I pictured all of us standing on the beach barefoot in our colorful dresses with our husbands to be before us. Travis is emotional, holding back his tears from meeting his mother for the first time. I still had concerns about how he would react and can only hope it will be good.

My thoughts were interrupted by my phone ringing. I sat up and glanced at the screen. It was Jill.

"Hey Jill, what's up?"

"Did Claire call you? She talked to Travis's mom. I'm so excited. I told her to invite her to the wedding."

I laughed at Jill's excitement. "Yes, she called me, and I agreed she should invite her. She sounds nice from what Claire told, but man, she's had a rough life."

"Yeah. I feel bad for her."

"Well, let's hope we can all be her new family."

"That would be awesome. I really hope this all works out, and she keeps in touch with them." Jill quickly changed the subject. "Down Maggie! Down."

I laughed.

"I'm sorry. Maggie still thinks she is a puppy. She's not." Jill squealed. She is growing so fast. But I love her."

"She is a cutie," I agreed.

I suddenly remembered my conversation with Slater last night. "Hey, I talked to Slater about a bachelor party."

"Oh, you did? What did he say? Are the guys doing something? I forgot to ask Ricky. He is working so much and is so dog-tired when he gets home. After sex, he is out like a light." She giggled.

"Ha! Glad to hear he is staying awake for sex. No, Slater said the guys haven't talked about anything, but I told him about my idea of us all doing something together, and he actually prefers it over us women going someplace on our own."

Jill sounded surprised. "Really."

"Yeah. I even told him that we ladies might have a surprise for them."

I detected the confusion in Jill's voice. "We do? How come I don't know anything about it? How can I surprise someone if I have no idea what I am surprising them with?"

"Well, I have this idea that I want to run by you and Claire, and you can tell me what you think? I think it will be fun, and I know the guys will love it."

I pictured Jill's eyes growing wide. "Ooh, do tell."

I told Jill my idea and waited anxiously for her reaction.

"I friggin love it. And you are right; the guys will love it too."

I was thrilled that Jill loved my pitch. "You do? Awesome. Do you think Claire will? She seems more reserved. I'm not sure if she will like it."

Jill laughed. "Yeah, she might need a little more persuasion. When are you going to ask her?"

"I can call her back after I've finished talking to you. If we are going to do this, I want to do it soon before I get too big. I feel like I'm gaining a pound a day. My boobs are getting huge."

"Oh, I bet Slater is loving that." Jill laughed and then added. "I want to give you a baby shower. All of this has to happen before our wedding. We only have four months until the twins are born and six months until our wedding. We have to get cracking. I'm going to go so you can call Claire. Call me back after you have talked to her."

"Will do. Bye."

Jill was right. Claire wasn't sold on the idea right away.

"Oh, I don't know, Sabela. I'd just be doing it for Travis, right? No kinky stuff?"

"Yes, Claire. No kinky stuff. I'll be with Slater. You'll be with Travis, and Jill will be with Ricky. We won't be switching or doing anything kinky, as you put it."

There was silence, and I gave her a little nudge. "Come on, Claire, it will be fun. We only plan on getting married once, and we'd be all partying together and carrying on the tradition by all getting married on the same day."

Claire released a small chuckle. "I've never done anything like that before. I don't know if I'd be any good at it. What if Travis laughs at me?"

"He won't laugh at you. He loves you. Look at me. I'm fat and pregnant, and I'm going to do it."

"Oh, but you are gorgeous. Even pregnant. And besides, you are not that big. And Jill is a knockout."

"Will you stop comparing all of us? Our guys love us for who we are. You are beautiful inside and out. It's why Travis loves you. You know the men will love this if we do it."

There was silence again. "Okay, I'll do it. But I have to practice. How long do I have?" She said with a laugh and then burst into a panic. "Wait! Will we all be in the same room?"

"We want to do it soon before I get too big. These babies are growing fast, and yes, we will be in the same room."

Claire's tone became more serious. "Oh, I don't know, Sabela. It's bad enough I'll be doing this in front of Travis but you and Jill too, and not to mention Ricky and Slater."

I laughed at her nervousness. "Claire, It will be fun. Just concentrate on Travis. You won't even know we are there."

"Easy for you to say."

I sensed she still needed a little push. "So you'll do it?"

There was silence, and then she spoke. "Yes, I'll do it. I can't believe I'm saying yes."

"Great! Let me call Jill back, and we will figure out a date. This is going to be so much fun. I can't wait to see the guys' faces."

I immediately called Jill back.

"Well?" she asked.

"She will do it." I squealed down the phone.

"She will! Wow, I never thought she would."

"Well, you were right. It did take some persuasion, but she finally said yes. How about the weekend after next? I'm meeting my mom for lunch this Saturday, and I can ask her if she wants Scottie for the weekend. I thought we could do it at our place."

"Sounds good to me. Gives me a chance to go shopping."

"Me too."

After hanging up the phone, I noticed my headache had gone, and I no longer felt nauseated. So much is going on. I don't have time to be down for a day and headed up to the office to do some work.

CHAPTER 21

The week flew by, and everything was falling into place. I couldn't believe how well it was going. I was waiting for something to go terribly wrong, and amazingly, nothing had.

Claire and Travis had been working diligently on everything needed for the foster home. Claire had completed her classes, and they approved the permits for a foster home and an adoption agency. After the wedding and when they returned from their honeymoon, which they had yet to decide on, they would move into the house and welcome their first child.

Jill called her parents, and she was right. They didn't mention anything about helping with the wedding plans. They would be flying in a day before the wedding, staying in a hotel close by, leaving the morning after the wedding, and flying back to Spain. Jill also told me that Ricky hadn't had time to call his family yet, but would make time this weekend. I hadn't thought about it until Jill mentioned it, but it would be the first time Jill met Ricky's parents and his sister. "I'm really nervous. I hope they like me," Jill said.

"Why wouldn't they, Jill?" I had told her. "You are beautiful, and you and Ricky make such a great couple."

"I kind of wish I was in Travis's shoes. He's not nervous at all about meeting his mom for the first time."

"Well, that's because he doesn't know Jill," I explained.

"Exactly. I wish this could be a surprise, and I wouldn't have all these anxieties."

I laughed at her reasoning. "Oh, Jill, everything is going to be just fine. Quit worrying so much. I'm sure you will all get along wonderfully. And don't forget, Ricky will be meeting your parents for the first time too," I reminded her. "I'm sure he is feeling somewhat nervous also. Has he said anything?"

"Nah, and he has nothing to worry about. My parents are so invested in themselves, even I feel like I don't know them," Jill joked.

Other than our immediate family and a few close friends, including Sadie and Slater's old boss, Drew, it would be a small gathering on the beach, with more people invited to the reception after the wedding ceremony.

I checked the clock on the kitchen wall from where I sat at the table, drinking a fruit smoothie. Slater and Scottie had already left for the Saturday T-ball game, and I had a few hours to myself before meeting my mom for lunch. Just enough time to take a shower, do my hair, and get ready.

I arrived at the Italian restaurant ten minutes early, surprised to see my mom already waiting at a table.

"Hey, mom, have you been here long?" I asked, taking a seat across from her in the booth.

"No, I just got here a few minutes ago. Traffic was light."

I couldn't help noticing how good my mom looked. Since dad died, she let herself go a little bit, but today her hair shined with a new chestnut color, and the streaks of grey disappeared. She was wearing more makeup than usual—eyeliner and thicker mascara.

Her lips beamed a rosy pink lipstick, and it well defined her cheeks with the hint of rouge blush she wore. "Mom, you look fantastic."

She glanced down at her forest green dress and smoothed it with her hands. "Thanks, I just bought this last week."

"It looks great on you. And I love the black belt. It really sets off the whole dress."

The waiter approached our table with two menus and took our drink order. Mom asked for a glass of Chablis, and I ordered an unsweetened iced tea.

"Did you have a make-over, mom?" I asked after the waiter had left. "I can't get over how great you look."

My mom giggled. "Well, as a matter of fact, I did have my hair done." She fluffed her hair as she spoke. "And I treated myself to some new clothes and just thought it was time I started taking care of myself again."

The waiter returned with our drinks, and after giving him our order, mom took a sip of her wine before she spoke. "I wanted to have lunch with you because I wanted to ask you something."

She looked worried when she made her announcement, and I became concerned. "Sure, what's up, mom?"

She hesitated before she answered and played with the stem of the glass. I didn't want to rush her and waited patiently for her reply.

"Would you mind if I bring a friend to the wedding?"

"Of course not mom, do I know her?"

Mom corrected me. "It's a he."

I was surprised when she told me, and I'm sure my jaw dropped. "Oh, Well, do I know him?"

"As a matter of fact, you do. It's Lorenzo from the bakery."

This time I knew my jaw dropped, and I quickly closed my mouth and tried to hide my shocked reaction, knowing I had failed. "Lorenzo, the Italian guy that kept flirting with you?" I gave her a big smile.

My mom blushed, "yes."

I leaned back in the booth. It suddenly all made sense—moms' new hairdo and wardrobe. "Wait, are you dating?"

She shook her head vigorously. "No, no, we are just friends," and then added, "really good friends. I like him a lot, but…"

"But what, mom?"

She closed her eyes and clasped her hands in front of her on the table. "I feel guilty, Sabela. I was married to your father for over twenty-five years. I still love him, and I miss him so much." Tears pooled in her eyes.

I reached across the table and placed my hands on top of hers. "Oh, mom, of course, you love dad. And I'm sure you miss him every day. I do, but it doesn't mean you have to stop living. No one will ever replace dad. He will always be your first love and hold a special place in our hearts. But you don't have to spend the rest of your life alone. Just because you're seeing Lorenzo doesn't mean you don't love dad." Something occurred to me. "Wait, didn't Lorenzo lose his wife too?"

My mom nodded. "Yes, the same year I lost your father."

"Does he talk about her often? Do you talk about dad to him?"

She nodded again. "Yes, we do. We share our grief and cry on each other's shoulders. It really is quite wonderful to share and be understood by someone who has experienced the same kind of loss. I think that is why we get along so well. When I went to his store by myself for the cake tasting appointment, we really hit it off. I was there for hours, and the next night we went out for dinner, and since then, we have spent a lot of time together—long walks in the park. We had dinner one evening at a piano bar, and he took me to the botanical gardens. It's been just wonderful." She gave me a snarky grin. "I want you to know I have not slept with him."

"I laughed. "Mom, I don't need to know those kinds of details." It stunned me that my mom had been spending so much time with Lorenzo, and I never knew it. "But how come you never told me?"

"I was afraid you would be mad or upset. You've only known me to be with your father."

"Oh, mom, I love you. I'm thrilled for you. I'm always so worried about you being alone. Dad would approve. Trust me, he would want you to be happy, and I can see that you are. Look at you. You are taking care of yourself again and going places. I would love it if you bring him to the wedding."

My mom's eyes lit up, "really! Oh, Sabela, thank you. He really is a wonderful man. He makes me happy, but in a different way. There will never be anyone like your father."

I gave her hand a gentle squeeze. "I know that, mom. I'm so happy you found each other. You are both supporting each other and bringing each other happiness after losing your spouses. I think it's beautiful."

The waiter came to our table with a handful of food. "Now come on, let's eat," I said with a smile.

CHAPTER 22

*N*ow that I knew about my mom's secret friendship with Lorenzo, she couldn't wait to call me a few times during the week to tell me about their latest date. She sounded so happy when we spoke, and I could picture her big smile when she told me about her latest adventure with him.

When I went to my mom's house on Friday afternoon to drop off Scottie for the weekend, I was surprised when Lorenzo answered the door. "Hi Lorenzo, is my mom home?"

He greeted me with a huge hug and a peck on the cheek, "Si, senora. She is stirring my spaghetti." He waved me in. "Come in and smell the good food cooking."

"Wow, it smells really good." He was right. The delicious aroma hit me as soon as I entered the house.

Scottie instantly let go of my hand and ran through the house to the kitchen where he was greeted by mom with a dozen kisses.

"Hey mom, something smells delicious."

She turned and smiled, holding a wooden spoon in her hand. "Lorenzo makes the best spaghetti". She dipped the spoon in the sauce. "Here, you have to try this."

I took the spoon and gave the sauce a quick blow before putting it in my mouth. "Wow, that is delicious."

Lorenzo laughed. "Si." Lorenzo kissed his fingers and waved them in the air. "Lorenzo makes the best spaghetti. It's my mama's recipe. Handed three generations down. Please, stay for dinner?" He insisted.

I shook my head. "No, I'm sorry I can't. I have to get ready for tomorrow. We are having a little get-together with friends at our place instead of doing a bachelorette party or bachelor party."

"What a great idea," mom said while still holding onto Scottie. She rubbed the top of his head. "We are going to take this little guy to the zoo tomorrow."

Scottie's eyes lit up, "really! We are going to the zoo?"

My mom pinched his cheek and freed him of her hold. "Yes, we are." She glanced over at Lorenzo and smiled. "Lorenzo is taking us. He is my new friend."

"Cool," Scottie said before scurrying off to his toy chest in the front room.

"Well, I don't think I will be missed." I laughed and hugged my mom. Have fun. I'll see you Sunday afternoon. Why don't you come to our house for dinner and that way Slater can meet Lorenzo. He's dying to meet him."

Lorenzo took my mom in his arms and kissed her gently on the cheek. It made me smile.

He grinned. "Gracie's. Thank you so much."

My mom wrapped her arms around Lorenzo's waist. "We will see you on Sunday."

After leaving my mom's house, I headed to the market to grab the fixings for tomorrow's dinner. I wanted everything to be perfect. Claire and Jill planned on being at my house by three so we could all pitch in making the planned meal of beef Wellington cooked with fresh vegetables. It was Claire's recipe that she had gotten from her mom but never tried it. It sounded fantastic. Filet mignon wrapped in a flaky pastry and baked in the oven. Dessert was going to be champagne and chocolate-dipped strawberries and apple cider for Travis and me.

We had been in contact via phone all week, planning our big surprise for our men. Jill was dying to tell Ricky, but Claire and I swore her to secrecy.

"Imagine the look on his face Saturday night." I had reminded her. "It's going to be well worth it. Please don't say anything to him." I pleaded, and so far, as hard as it has been to not tell, Ricky and the others had no clue. All they knew was that we were getting together for dinner at our place. Jill, Claire, and I also agreed not to show our outfits to each other.

"We will be as surprised as our men." I had said when I called yesterday to make sure they had purchased theirs. They had, and I had bought mine two days ago when Scottie was in school and tucked it away in the back of my closet.

After returning home from the store, I was relieved to find the house empty. Slater was still working. I checked my phone to see if I had missed a text from him and saw that I had not. I had an hour to put the food away and do some last-minute preparations for our surprise tomorrow. I giggled when I thought of the men's reaction and knew this was a much better idea than the traditional bachelor and bachelorette parties.

CHAPTER 23

As per our plan, Claire called Slater on his phone the next day. I turned away and smiled to myself as Slater picked up his phone.

"Hey, Claire, what's up?"

I knew what Claire was saying and pretended I didn't when he ended the call. By now, Claire should be calling Ricky.

"Is everything okay?" I asked.

"I hope so. Claire asked if I wouldn't mind hanging out with Travis for a few hours while she ran some errands. She told me he was feeling a little under the weather and would probably love some company. She is going to ask Ricky too."

"Oh, okay."

"Yeah, she thinks hanging with the guys will do him some good. Would you mind?"

I gave him a loving smile. "Of course not, sweetie, it will give me some time to get ready for our dinner tonight."

"Great, let me grab a few things, and I will see you this afternoon." He gave me a cute grin. "So, what's on the menu for tonight?"

I wrapped my arms around his waist and gave him a long smooch on the lips. "It's a surprise."

"Ooh, I love surprises, and I love you."

After he left, I immediately called Claire and Jill and told them the coast was clear. Within an hour, they were at my house. Their outfits, hidden in bags, were stashed in my closet next to mine.

Jill connected her phone to my Bluetooth sound system and blasted the apartment with Madonna music while washing and cleaning the strawberries. Claire and I set the table with flowers, my best crystal, and dinnerware, and we danced around the kitchen as we prepped the vegetables.

"This is a brilliant idea." Jill squealed as she put the large bowl of strawberries in the fridge. "I can't wait to see the men's faces," she laughed.

"I still can't believe you talked me into this," Claire joked. "Do you know how many hours I have spent practicing in front of the mirror?" She laughed and stole a strawberry from the bowl before Jill closed the fridge door. "And I still don't like what I see," she added. "I'm telling you, Travis is going to laugh at me."

"No, he's not. You are going to knock his socks off." I threw back my head and cracked a loud laugh.

Jill swayed her hips and danced across the kitchen. "I've been practicing too." She gave us a sultry stare. "And let me tell you, when Ricky and I go home tonight, he is not getting any sleep. We are going to make love until the sun comes up."

"Well, I'm sure after our surprise, Travis and Ricky are not going to want to stick around. They are going to want to get you ladies home as quickly as humanly possible. I'll be kicking you out anyway. I have plans for Slater and me," I said with a giggle and a wink.

Once everything was in place, I took a break on the couch and rubbed my stomach. "I'm sure glad we are doing the surprise this weekend while I still have some moves left in me."

Claire and Jill joined me. "Are they kicking yet?" Jill asked as she placed her hand on my stomach.

"No, not yet. I'm five months along. I should feel them any day now."

"Gosh, I can't wait to meet them. I want to have a baby shower next month." Jill announced.

I hesitated before speaking. "Jill, I love that you want to do that, but do you mind if we wait a few more months?."

Jill creased her brow. "Why?"

I released a heavy sigh. "This may sound stupid, but I want to make sure there are no risks with my pregnancy. Twins tend to have more complications. As more time goes by, I know they are growing and becoming stronger. I don't want to jinx anything." I chuckled. "Maybe I'm a little superstitious."

"I agree with her," Claire replied.

Jill failed to hide her disappointment with her defeated tone. "Okay, I guess. Well, it gives me more time to plan it."

I smiled. "Thank you." I grabbed my phone off the coffee table and checked the time. "It's almost two. We told the guys dinner would be at five." I turned to Claire. "So you are going to head home so Ricky and Slater can leave, right?"

Claire nodded. "Yes, I'll put on a nice dinner outfit, and we will be back here at four to help you fix dinner." She looked over at Jill. "You have to be here at four with Ricky?"

"Yes, we'll be here," Jill said, turning down the music a notch with her phone.

I clapped my hands together and squealed. "Oh, this is going to be so much fun; I can't wait." I stood from the couch. "Okay, now get out of here. I need to take a shower and get ready."

Slater arrived home within the hour. I had just finished taking a shower and came downstairs dressed in my bathrobe.

He met me at the bottom of the stairs and took me in his arms. His warm lips met mine, and I found his tongue. "Mmm, you smell good."

I pressed my body against his and breathed in his scent. "So do you," kissing him again. "I love you so much."

Slater gave me that smile that always melted my heart and gently untied the belt to my robe, allowing it to open freely and expose my naked body. He glanced down and placed his hand gently on my breast. His touch made my skin tingle, and I closed my eyes as he caressed my breasts with both of his hands. "God, and I love you."

I wrapped my arms around his neck and threw back my head with my eyes closed as he opened my robe a little more and began kissing my stomach and tracing my skin with his tongue. "I can't believe how lucky I am," he whispered between kisses. "You make me so happy."

I leaned in and kissed the top of his head and buried my face in his hair as he continued to caress my body. "And you make me so happy, too. Every day I feel like I am living a dream." I cupped his chin with my fingers and pulled his head up towards me, and gazed into his eyes. "Kiss me."

Slater raised his head to meet my lips and devoured my mouth with a long, sensual kiss as he embraced me in his arms. We remained locked with our tongues entwined until we had to break for air.

"You never cease to take my breath away," Slater panted. "If we weren't having guests over tonight, I'd be carrying you up to the bedroom right about now."

I kissed him again as I closed my robe and tied the belt. I spoke in a flirty manner. "There is always later."

He took my hand and led me down the last step. "I'm going to hold you to that. Hey, the table looks amazing. What's for dinner?"

"It's a surprise. Now, why don't you take a shower while I finish getting ready."

A half-hour before everyone was due to arrive, I began feeling the excitement of the evening's events. It filled me with nervous energy, but in a good way. I dressed in my black flared mini dress, which I was thankful I had a stretchy waistline and still fit. After giving my hair a good shake and tease, I admired how full it looked flowing down my back. I sat on the edge of the bed to put on my matching black heels and glanced in the mirror to check my makeup and the black choker around my neck—one of Slater's favorite pieces of jewelry that I owned. I smiled at my reflection, feeling satisfied with my appearance, and headed downstairs to join Slater.

I found him with a beer in his hand, browsing his phone on the couch. He had not heard me enter, and I admired him from across the room. The scent of his sweet-smelling cologne filled the air, and I breathed it in. I loved the smell. He was dressed in faded jeans that fit him perfectly and hugged his toned legs. The crisp white shirt he wore with the sleeves rolled up mid way was unbuttoned just enough to tease his tanned chest and muscular arms. A silver chain hung around his neck, and his wavy chestnut hair swayed slightly from the breeze from the air conditioner vent blowing above the couch.

"You look gorgeous," I said with a smile as I approached him.

He looked up, and a huge smile appeared on his face. "Wow, you are a knockout." He stood and took my hand, raised it, and twirled me. "You are stunning. How soon can I take that dress off you?" he joked.

I gave his chest a friendly pat and teased him. "After our guests have left."

Slater grabbed my waist and pulled me in for a kiss. "Let's make it a quick dinner." He chuckled.

I pulled away from his embrace and laughed. "I'm off to the kitchen. Why don't you finish your beer and wait for the guys to arrive? Claire and Jill will be helping me in the kitchen."

The others arrived a few minutes apart and looked stunning, especially Claire. I'd never seen her so dolled up and wearing more makeup than usual. Her lips were super luscious painted red, and the eyeliner and black mascara looked super sexy.

"Wow, Claire, look at you," I screamed as she walked through the door and did a twirl to show off her red mini dress and matching pumps. "And you are not wearing glasses," I added.

"I am wearing contacts, and they are killing me," she whispered. "I'm not sure how long I can keep them in."

"Well, I think glasses are sexy. They make you look smart. Not saying you aren't, mind you."

Travis had been standing behind Claire while I admired her wardrobe. "Doesn't she look great? I love that red lipstick she is wearing. It's the third time she's put it on this afternoon. I keep kissing it off her." Travis laughed as he closed the door behind him and headed over to the fridge to grab a beer.

"Grab me one too," Claire hollered. "Make it two," she joked under her breath.

"Claire! Do you plan on getting drunk tonight?"

"I plan on being drunk before our surprise. I need alcohol courage. I'm a nervous wreck."

I rested my hand on her shoulder. "Oh, stop, you will be great. I see Travis is having a beer, too. Is that okay?"

"Yeah, he's off the meds, and he only has one now and then. He's not drinking like he used to."

I led Claire into the kitchen when there was another knock at the door. "That must be Jill and Ricky. I'll be right back."

Claire took a beer from Travis as he walked by to join Slater while I greeted Jill and Ricky.

As soon as I opened the door, I was deafened by Jill's high pitch squeal and found myself wrapped in her arms. "We are here. I'm so excited."

I nodded at Ricky from her embrace as he walked by and joined Slater and Travis, who already had a beer on the coffee table for him. I pulled away from Jill's arms and admired her pink pastel tight-fitting dress and white heels. "I love your dress, Jill."

She smiled. "Thanks, I like the one upstairs better," she giggled.

While the men hung out in the front room talking about whatever guys talked about, we got to work in the kitchen. Claire was in charge of preparing the Beef Wellington, seeing how it was her family's recipe, while Jill and I did the finishing touches to the table and put the vegetables in the pan. Within fifteen minutes, dinner was cooking in the oven.

Jill grabbed her phone off the table. "Let's dance," she said, while tapping her phone. A few seconds later, Jennifer Lopez blasted from the surround sound speakers. "Hey, Ricky." Jill hollered across the room. "Come dance with me."

Ricky starred in her direction, smiled, and took a swig of his beer as he watched Jill give him some sexy dance moves from across the room. "I'm on my way, baby."

Claire and I watched them for a few minutes as they were lost in each other's eyes and arms, kissing passionately while moving in tune to the music.

I glanced over at Slater and Travis. Both were watching Jill and Ricky. "Come on, guys. There are two lonely women here that want to dance," I said, followed by a wink at Slater.

The two men quickly stood and trotted over to us. Slater swayed his hips as he walked and gave me a luring smile. I met him halfway and embraced his masculine body. For some time, we danced with our loved ones. I would look over and see Travis whisper something in Claire's ear that she obviously liked. She giggled, whispered something back in his ear before kissing him hard on the lips. Jill had her hands on Ricky's butt and massaged it vigorously before pulling him in closer. We were all so in love, and it was beautiful to see. Let the fun begin.

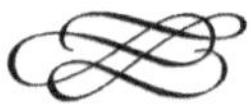

CHAPTER 25

*D*inner was a success, and after Claire and Jill helped me clear the table, I turned and gave our men a sultry smile. "So guys, are you ready for dessert?"

Slater beamed at me with a smile. "Sure, what are we having?"

I glanced across the table at Jill, who giggled and released a tiny feminine snort. "Are you ready, ladies?"

Jill looked over at Ricky and circled her lips with her tongue. "You bet I am."

"Let's do this," Claire added as she took a large gulp of her beer.

Obviously, the men knew we were up to something when they gave us a suspicious look and narrowed their eyes with a furrowed brow.

I stood first. Claire and Jill immediately followed while failing to hide their mischievous smiles.

"Okay, guys, we have a little surprise for you. Why don't you all head over to the couch for a few minutes," I told them.

The men gave one another a confused look and a nervous smile, but went along with our game. As soon as their chairs were free, we each grabbed one and lined them up about four feet apart at one end of the front room.

Slater looked over his shoulder at the three chairs while I went to a kitchen drawer. "What are you girls up to?" Slater asked, followed by a chuckle.

"You'll see." Jill giggled before blowing Ricky a kiss.

"Found them." I hollered from the kitchen and hid them behind my back as I walked back to the chairs.

"Found what?" Travis questioned with another nervous laugh.

Claire and Jill walked slowly over to our three puzzled men, wearing devious smiles, and held out their hands.

"Why don't you three come take a seat on the chairs," Jill said, pulling Ricky up from the couch. Claire did the same.

"You too, Slater," I called from where I stood, using my index finger and narrowed eyes to call him over.

Once the men were sitting in their chairs, we stood behind them, and it was then that I handed Claire and Jill a set of hand-cuffs that I had been hiding behind my back. "Here you go, ladies."

Jill giggled loudly. "Thank you."

At the same time, we all leaned over and grabbed the men's wrists, pulled them behind the back of the chairs, and snapped the handcuffs into place.

"Hey, what are you doing?" The men all said at the same time with a dropped jaw and eyes wide.

Jill pulled Ricky's head back, bent over, and gave him a hard kiss on the lips. "You'll see."

Travis released a nervous laugh and glanced over at Slater, who shrugged his shoulders and grinned. "Claire, what are you up to?"

Claire reached over and ran her hand down his chest. "It's a surprise, sweetie."

I laughed at the men's nervous laughs and whispered in Slater's ear, making sure Travis and Ricky heard too. "We will be right back."

Slater jolted and strained to turn his head. "What? You are going to leave us here?"

Jill laughed the loudest as we headed for the stairs.

I turned and smiled. "It's just for a little while." I wet my lips with my tongue. "Now, don't go anywhere."

Once we were in my bedroom, I quickly closed the door and joined Claire and Jill in a burst of laughter. Jill had already collapsed onto the bed, gripping her stomach from laughing so hard.

"Did you see their faces?" she bellowed. "Oh, I wish I had a photo. It was classic."

"I wonder what they are thinking?" Claire said as she grabbed her bag from my closet."

I grabbed my bag and handed Jill hers. "Wait till we go back downstairs. I can't wait to see their faces then." I opened up my bag and poured the contents onto the bed. "Hey Jill, did you remember to bring your phone?"

"Yes, it's right here," Jill said, waving her hand.

"Good, you can change the music just before we make our entrance," I told her. "Okay, let's get changed."

With limited space, we scrambled, giggling the entire time to change into our sexy, seductive outfits. "I love the schoolgirl outfit," I told Jill as she stood in front of the full-length mirror, tying her hair into pigtails and adding a red bow to the end of each one. She twirled and gave her boobs an extra push in the white lace bra to reveal extra cleavage.

"Undo one more button on your shirt," I told her. "Let Ricky see your boobs and some of that pretty lace bra."

Jill didn't hesitate and quickly revealed more bosom before adjusting the ties on the white shirt just beneath her breast line. She smoothed out her red plaid ultra mini skirt and straightened out the waistline.

"What shoes are you wearing?" Claire asked Jill as she wriggled her body into a black corset that barely covered her chest.

Jill skipped over to the bed and pulled out a pair of vinyl white thigh boots with laces all the way to the top and six-inch heels. She grinned, "these."

"Wow, I love those." Claire laughed while pulling her corset tight and snapping the hooks together.

My jaw dropped as Claire's boobs met together in a sexy mound. She looked at herself in the mirror, wearing black lace panties and a corset. "You don't think it's too much?" she said, while giving her hair a hard shake.

"Hell no, you are a knockout." I screeched while pulling on my leather onesie that hid my pregnancy well. "What are you wearing on the bottom?" I asked Claire.

Claire grabbed a black mini skirt from the top of the dresser. I have this skirt, a pair of black fishnet stockings and army boots. She then held up a black leather choker with fake diamond studs. "And I have this too."

"Oh, you are going to blow Travis's socks off." Jill squealed while sitting on the edge of the bed, tying her boots.

Once I had the onesie on, I joined Jill on the edge of the bed, rolled black fishnet stocking up my leg, and then grabbed my black thigh boots off the bed.

"Those are like mine, but black," Jill said as she stood up and admired herself in the mirror.

I pulled one leg into the boot and laced it up. "They are."

Once both boots were on, I walked over to the dresser and adjusted Slater's favorite black choker, and gave my hair a good tease. I looked in the mirror and loved what I saw. The leather onesie fit perfectly, hugging my body, showing every curve. The V-neck in front was low, almost to my belly button, with leather straps across my breast. Being pregnant, my breasts were round and full and came together in a seductive, sultry way.

"You look fantastic," Claire said as she joined me in front of the mirror.

I put my arm around her waist and admired our reflection in

the mirror. "So do you. Travis's eyes are going to fall out," I laughed.

Jill giggled from behind us and came and stood on my other side. Our arms wrapped around each other's waist, and we all stared into the mirror and smiled. There was no denying it. We all looked hot. "Well, ladies, are we ready to seduce our men and give them a night to remember?"

"Oh hell yes," Jill shouted. "Let's do this."

Claire and Jill followed me to the door, and after I had opened it, Jill tapped some buttons on her phone and gave me a nod. The surround sound suddenly went silent, and I heard Ricky speak.

"What happened? The music went off?"

"I dunno?" Travis replied.

We giggled from upstairs with our hands to our mouths as we waited for the music to come back on. A few seconds later, the song "Good For You" by Selena Gomez blasted through the speakers, and that was our cue.

Jill went down the stairs first, followed by Claire and then me. All of us wore seductive smiles and strutted in a sexy manner, swaying our hips to the erotic beat of the music. We gave the men a luring stare and circled our lips with our tongues.

"Are you ready for your desserts, boys?" Jill purred as she reached the bottom stair.

Slater, Ricky, and Travis strained to turn their necks. Their eyes were wide, and their jaws dropped.

Ricky spoke first. "Wow, I think I have just gone to heaven."

"Holy shit, Claire, you are a knockout," Travis grinned

I matched Slater's huge grin as I cat walked over to him, leaned in, and whispered in his ear. "How are you doing, baby?"

"Friggin fantastic, kiss me."

I placed my finger on his lips. "Shh, all in good time. First, enjoy the show."

I looked over at Claire and saw she was a fast learner. If she was nervous, she was doing a damn good job of hiding it. Travis couldn't take his eyes off her as she danced provocatively before him. She pushed her breasts close to his face and massaged his chest with her slow-moving hands.

Jill was all over Ricky—kissing every inch of bare skin, his lips, neck, and the exposed part of his chest. Ricky kissed her back like a hungry dog, enjoying the tease. God, they looked hot.

I turned my attention back to Slater and moved my body with intentions to seduce, curling my lips and shaking my hair in his face before I turned around and swayed my butt from side to side while thrusting my hips where my hands rested. I looked over my shoulder and smiled at him before moistening my lips again and giving my ass a loud smack.

Slater moaned. "God, you are sexy."

I turned to face him, tilted my head, and tossed my hair back away from my face. "Yeah, you like what you see?"

"Hell yes," Slater said, with eyes lit up like a boy in a candy store.

I ran my hands over his shirt and down to the bulge in his pants. "And I like this." I gave it a gentle squeeze. "Now, wait right here while we get dessert."

"I thought this was dessert," Slater said with a slight moan.

I brushed my finger across his lips. "Oh, baby, we are just getting started."

"Ladies, it's time to bring out the dessert."

Jill and Claire came to an abrupt stop and giggled at their men.

"We will be right back," Jill whispered to Ricky, who shifted in his seat.

"But you can't stop now," he whined.

Jill giggled as she followed me to the kitchen, locking arms with Claire. The giggles continued in the kitchen as we each grabbed a champagne glass of chocolate-covered strawberries and strutted back to our men.

The music had changed to Cream by Prince, and I lip-synced the words to the song as I straddled Slater and ground my body against his. *"Cream gets on top."* I sang into Slater's ear as I pressed my body against his and kissed him hard on the lips. Our tongues met, and I devoured his mouth and mated with his tongue. "I'm so turned on right now. I can't wait to get you in bed." I whispered, before holding a strawberry close to his lips.

Slater tilted back his head and opened his mouth, taking a bite. I kissed him again with the fruit in his mouth and let the juices flow into mine. Slater pulled away, panting, and buried his head into my bosom. I thrust my hips again and rubbed my full breast from side to side across his face. My moves were exotic and slow. My breathing was heavy, and my chest heaved as I felt the warmth of his breath teasing my skin. Before kissing him again, I peeked over at Jill and Claire.

Each engaged heavily with their men. Feeding them strawberries as they straddled on their laps. Their arms were either around the guy's neck or exploring their chests with long, deep strokes of their free hand. Jill had unbuttoned Ricky's shirt and was now licking his bare skin with her tongue while Ricky moaned with pleasure.

Claire had a strawberry halfway in her mouth and leaned in so Travis could steal it in a kiss. With the strawberry in his mouth, she leaned back and caressed her breast while tossing her hair from side to side. She then stood and showed off her behind to Travis with proactive moves while smiling over her shoulder. Travis's eyes were glued to the Claire he had never seen before—seeping lust.

We continued to tease our men with flirtatious moves and kisses to entice them. Jill was the first to stand after feeding Ricky a strawberry wedged between her breasts. After he had engulfed the fruit, Jill pulled out a shiny key and quickly stood to her feet.

"I want you. I'm taking you home," she said in bated breath and freed him from his cuffs.

Ricky quickly stood and took her in his arms, and met her in a fiery kiss. While still embraced, they turned and faced us and circled their lips. Jill ran her hand through her hair and kissed Ricky as he tried to speak and hide the prominent bulge in his pants. "We are out of here, guys. I have plans for my girl."

Jill giggled. "I can't wait," dragging him to the front door.

"Do you want to go home, baby?" Claire whispered to Travis as she rocked on his lap.

Travis kissed her passionately on the lips. "Hell yeah."

Claire undid a few of the top clasps on her corset and shook her breast vigorously until a key fell into their laps. She looked up and smiled at Travis before unlocking his cuffs.

Travis immediately stood. Rubbed his wrists and pulled Claire in close. "You are so damn hot. I can't wait to get you home."

Claire grabbed his hand. "Well, what are you waiting for?" She looked over his shoulder and winked at Slater and me. "Goodnight, guys. Thanks, it was fun. We are going to finish the party at home."

I beamed them a huge smile and waved. "Have fun."

"So, are you going to take these cuffs off of me so I can have my way with you?" Slater said, once the house was empty.

I gave him a mischievous grin. "Maybe I'm not done teasing you yet."

Slater closed his eyes and shook his head. "Oh sweetie, if you tease me anymore, I'll explode."

I leaned in and licked his ear.

Slater moaned. "You are killing me."

I blew into his ear. "Do you want me?"

"Yes," Slater laughed. "Set me free, woman."

"The key to freedom." I laughed, while still nibbling on his ear, I reached down in between my boobs and pulled out the key and dangled it in front of his face. I leaned in, pressing my breast hard against his chest, and kissed him with force. When I broke away for air, my chest was pounding, and my body was on fire. I stood and released Slater from the cuffs and let them fall to the floor.

Within seconds, his arms devoured me. His warm breath sent

tingles through my entire body. I didn't know if I could make it upstairs before ripping off my clothes. "Come on. I want to feel every inch of you. I want you inside of me now."

I grabbed his hand and pulled him towards the stairs.

"Woman, I am going to make love to you until I have no more to give."

CHAPTER 26

I nudged Slater lying next to me in a sound sleep. "Slater, wake up."

My hand rested on my stomach, and I giggled when I felt it again. Slater stirred, but his eyes remained closed. I couldn't blame him for still sleeping. Last night and in the early hours of the morning, we made love. It was wild, loud, and beautiful, all at the same time. Having the house to ourselves, we unleashed like we hadn't in a long time. I nudged him again. "Slater, honey, the babies are kicking. Wake up."

Suddenly, his eyes jolted open, and he sat up wide awake. "You said babies. What's wrong?" he asked in a panic.

I chuckled. "The babies are fine. They are kicking." I took his hand and rested it on my stomach. "Hold your hand still and wait."

Slater's jaw dropped, "really." He waited a few seconds. "I don't feel anything."

"Just give it a minute," I whispered.

In silence, with his hands resting gently on my stomach, we patiently waited, and then I laughed when Slater gasped and shrieked. "Oh my god, did you feel that?"

I laughed again. "Yes, of course, I felt it. They are kicking me."

Slater kept his hand on my stomach. "I want to feel it again." A few seconds later, he shrieked again. "I just felt another kick. I wonder if it's just one or both of them kicking?"

"I'm assuming both, but who knows?" The babies kicked again. Slater and I laughed at the same time.

"This is friggin amazing," Slater said with a huge grin. "How does it feel? It has to feel really weird to be kicked from the inside out."

I laughed at his remark. "It feels kind of strange, but it also makes it surreal. Two little babies are growing inside me, and to feel them move and kick is such an out-of-this-world experience. I can't wait to be holding them." I curled into Slater's arms and rested my head on his chest. "Sometimes, I have to pinch myself. I can't believe we are having twins."

Slater kissed the top of my head. "Me either. Feeling them kick made it that more wonderful." He shifted and unwrapped himself from our embrace. "Why don't you relax, and I'll bring you some juice."

I shook my head and pulled the sheets away from my naked body. "No, I have a hard time relaxing. I cramp up if I'm motionless for too long. Oh, I forgot to tell you, with all the planning of the little surprise last night, mom is bringing Scottie home this afternoon with Lorenzo, and they are staying for dinner."

"Oh, good, I will finally get to meet him. Do you want me to barbecue?"

"Er, no, I thought about making chili and cornbread." One day I will tell him his cooking sucks, I promised myself. "It's much easier, and it's Scottie's favorite," I added.

"Okay, well, let me help, okay. I'm going to jump in the shower."

❀

When mom arrived, her smile told me the happiness she was experiencing with her newfound friendship. I knew in my heart dad would approve, and so would Lorenzo's late wife, Angelica.

It seemed Scottie had made a new friend too and learned some Italian words when he was away. Lorenzo was good with kids, but that was not a surprise when I learned from mom that he had five children of his own. All grown and scattered across the globe, but they all came together for the holidays.

Slater was, as always, the perfect gentleman, making Lorenzo feel at home. Mom and I prepared dinner together while I watched from across the room, Slater and Lorenzo getting to know each other over a glass of wine. Scottie sat at their feet in a pile of Legos, interrupting periodically with his newest creation. I looked across at my mom, who was stirring the beans and humming a tune. Her eyes seeped happiness when she looked back. It felt good knowing I no longer needed to worry about her.

CHAPTER 27

"This time next year, we will be celebrating your first Mother's Day," Claire said. I had her on speaker, and Slater yelled from the kitchen.

"That's right, and we will treat her like the queen she is," Slater called from the sink where he was washing dishes.

I looked over my shoulder and laughed. "And then I will get to treat you like a king on Father's day."

I shifted on the couch. It was getting more difficult to find a comfortable position. Now that I was seven and half months pregnant, I was feeling aches and pains. Sleeping was the hardest. I couldn't lay in the same position for too long and tossed and turned all night. And when I did finally doze off, a sharp kick awoke me to my ever-growing stomach from one of the twins. I was irritable with my discomfort with no relief and apologized to Slater often for my sharp tone or impatience. Thank god he never took offense to my rudeness and instead tried to calm me down.

"Are you seeing your parents today?" I asked Claire.

"No, they went away for the weekend."

"That's good. They are getting out-of-town once in a while. I'm sure it does them good. Do you know where they went?"

"No, mom said. Dad surprised her. Travis and I are just hanging out here. I have to tell you, though, because it's Mother's Day, I can't stop thinking about his mom."

"Are you going to tell him?"

"No, I really want to surprise him. She texted me and said she has her hotel booked and work gave her the time off."

"That's great. I can't wait to meet her. When does she get here?"

"The day before the wedding, we will all meet her on the beach a little before the ceremony." Claire changed the subject. "Are you seeing your mom?"

"Yes. Lorenzo is cooking a big meal at my mom's house, so we are heading over there in a few hours. His mom will be there too," I gasped.

"Sabela, are you okay?"

I gave my stomach a deep rub. 'Yeah, I was just kicked really hard in the stomach by one of the twins."

"Only six more weeks, Sabela, and they will be here."

"I know. I can't believe it. This is getting harder day by day." I gasped as I felt liquid running down my legs and quickly stood up. The couch was drenched. "Oh no!"

"What is it, Sabela?" Claire said, sounding alarmed.

"I think my water broke. Slater! Come quick. Claire, I have to go. I think I'm going into labor."

"Oh shit! Call me as soon as you can."

"I will, bye." I threw down the phone and glanced over at the kitchen. Slater was not there. "Slater!" I yelled before doubling over with severe stomach cramps.

Suddenly, I heard racing footsteps down the stairs. "I'm here. What's wrong?"

I gripped my stomach as I spoke. "My water broke. The couch is ruined. I think the babies are coming."

Slater's jaw dropped. "What? It's too early."

"I know. I'm going to call my doctor. It may be false labor. Call my mom. Tell her to keep Scottie another night. Thank god he is with her and not here."

After calling my mom, Slater joined me in the front room and held my hand as I listened to my doctor. I screamed in the middle of our conversation at what I believed to be a contraction invading my body. "Okay, we are on our way." I quickly ended the call. "She said to go to the hospital. She will meet us there."

"Does she think you are in labor?" Slater asked as he grabbed my purse and phone.

"She's not sure, but she said it's not uncommon for twins to be born prematurely."

Slater squeezed my hand tight and walked me slowly to the front door. Again, I had to heave my chest and hold my stomach as another pain shot through me. "God, I hope they are okay."

Slater sensed my fear and tried to calm me. "Everything is going to be just fine. Come on; we are almost to the truck."

Overcome with fear and pain, I had forgotten all about my mom. "What did my mom say?" I asked as Slater put the truck in reverse.

"She said she will keep Scottie as long as we need her to and to keep her posted from the hospital."

I nodded and closed my eyes. Slater reached over and rubbed my knee. "Are you doing okay?"

"Yeah, as long as I don't get the shooting pains. I wonder if they are contractions?"

"Who knows? We've never had a kid before," Slater chuckled, trying to add humor to the concerns we were having.

When we reached the hospital in record time, I gripped the door handle hard and let out a loud scream. Another pain shot through me. "Fuck! How long does this shit go on for?"

Slater squeezed my shoulder. "Hang in there and wait here. Let me find someone to help us."

Still feeling the excruciating pains, I simply nodded with a scrunched face.

Slater returned with a male hospital volunteer pushing a wheelchair for what seemed like hours and was probably only minutes. Before they reached the truck, I let out another loud moan. I was uncomfortable. My body ached from head to toe, and my back was on fire. No matter how much I changed positions, the pain haunted my entire body. I wiped my hand across my brow to remove the beads of sweat pouring off my forehead and raked my fingers through my drenched hair.

The volunteer waited behind Slater as he opened the door. "How are you doing, sweetie?" Slater asked with worry.

I held my stomach. "I don't know. I hope the babies are okay."

Slater leaned into the truck and took my hand while supporting me with his other as I slowly eased myself out of the truck.

The male volunteer approached me with a wheelchair. "Everything is going to be okay. We are going to get you checked in, call your doctor and see what's going on."

I lowered my body slowly into the wheelchair. "Thank you."

Slater held my hand tight as he walked at the same pace as the wheelchair being pushed.

"By the way, I'm Ed. How far along are you?"

"She's seven and a half months," Slater replied as I released another moan.

"Are the babies going to be okay?" I asked while trying to fight off the intense pain I was having.

Ed tried to ease my anxieties. "I'm sure everything is going to be fine."

After what seemed like an eternity and continued pain, they finally wheeled me to a room after after I had been checked in, with Slater close by my side. I was now crying, fearing for our babies and the unknown. I was scared, and when I looked into Slater's eyes, I could see his fear too. I admired him for holding it together while I was falling apart.

"It's going to be okay, hon."

A nurse entered the room and gave us a caring smile. "So you are having twins?"

I nodded. "Yes, but it's too early."

"Well, we are going to see what is going on. Your doctor is on her way. In the meantime, I want to take your vitals and see how the little ones are doing."

I took Slater's hand. "Can my fiancée stay?"

"Yes, of course."

Slater and I remained quiet while the nurse ran her tests and entered some notes into a tablet.

"Is everything okay?" Slater asked with a hard stare.

"Her water has broken, and her blood pressure is high."

"What does that mean?" Slater insisted.

"The doctor will decide, but in the meantime, I'm going to give her a shot of antibiotics to prevent any infections since her water has broken and hook her up to an IV so we can monitor her vitals."

Slater's eyes showed fear, and he was now sweating as much as me. "Are the babies and Sabela going to be okay?"

"I'm sure everything is going to be fine," the nurse replied while wheeling over a contraption and computer monitor. "Many twins are born early. Seven plus months is not uncommon." She said as she continued to hook me up to the IV and poke my skin.

"Yeah, our doctor mentioned that," I answered while watching my hand being stuck with three needles.

A familiar voice caught my attention, and I looked towards the door and smiled. It was my doctor.

"How are you doing, Sabela? I wasn't expecting to see you here until late June. I guess the twins are eager to meet mom and dad."

Slater gasped as he took in a deep breath. "Is she having the babies today?"

My doctor took the tablet and glanced at the screen. "Her blood pressure is high, which is a concern, and she is already in labor, which I don't think we can stop. The babies seem to be doing just fine, but I don't want to put them or Sabela under any stress."

"So, what are you saying?" Slater asked as he gently brushed my hair away from my forehead.

"I think it would be best if we deliver the babies by c-section."

"But isn't it too early? Will the babies be okay?" I asked as panic took over.

"Because they will be prematurely born and small, they will need oxygen therapy to help them breathe for a week or so. We will know more once the twins are born." Doctor Tracy replied.

Slater let go of my hand and paced the room while raking his hands through his hair. "And what about Sabela? Is she going to be okay? Will I be able to be in the room when the C-section is being performed?"

Doctor Tracy shook her head. "' I'm afraid not. She will have to be closely monitored, and there are many risks that are involved that I will go over with you. I want to do this now because of her high blood pressure, which can cause complications such as heart and kidney disease and a stroke—not to mention problems with the placenta and blood flow.

Slater's eyes grew wide. "Oh my god. How soon are we talking about?"

Doctor Tracy checked her watch. "Within the hour. I'm ordering an emergency c-section. Hang tight and a nurse will be in for her shortly."

Slater shook her hand. "Thank you doctor."

"Don't you worry. She is in good hands. Everything is going to be just fine."

After Doctor Tracy left, Slater sat on the edge of the bed and took my hand. "So, are you ready to be a mom?"

I managed to release a small giggle. "Are you ready?"

He leaned in and kissed my brow. "I am."

I squeezed his hand and raised it to my lips. Tears pooled in my eyes. "I just hope they are going to be okay."

CHAPTER 28

I kept hearing my name.

"Sabela. Sabela."

Was I dreaming? My head felt so heavy, and my throat was dry. I tried to open my eyes and then heard my name again.

"Sabela. Are you awake?"

I felt a hand holding mine. Was I awake? I didn't know. Where am I? I tried again to open my eyes, and this time they fluttered to adjust to the lights, and then I saw Slater. He was smiling down at me, and I felt him squeeze my hand.

"Sabela. It's Slater. Can you hear me?"

I suddenly remembered the twins, and my eyes popped open. "The babies. Are they okay?"

His smile instantly told me they were.

"They are doing fine. We have two sweet girls."

Tears flushed down my cheeks, and my body trembled with relief.

Slater spoke again. "Did you hear me? We have baby girls, and they are going to be okay."

"Have you seen them? Will I be able to hold them?" I pleaded.

Slater shook his head. "I haven't seen them yet. We will see them for the first time together. They are in the NICU ward. Because they were born early and they need oxygen therapy and need to be closely monitored."

A lump formed in my throat. "So I won't be able to hold them?"

"Not for about a week, sweetheart. They need to gain some strength and be able to breathe on their own and maintain their body temperatures. They are so tiny."

Slater sat on the edge of the bed and held me in his arms. I rested my head on his chest.

"How big are they?"

"One is three pounds twelve ounces, and the other is four pounds one ounce." He told me.

"We don't even have names for them yet. I thought we would have more time to choose names," I said, coughing. "My throat is so dry."

Slater leaned over to a tray next to the bed. "Here is some shaved ice." He held a spoonful in front of my face. "Open your mouth."

"Oh, that feels so good. Thank you." I said as the cool drops from the melting ice dribbled down my throat.

"Do you have any ideas for names?" Slater asked as he fed me more ice.

I shook my head. "No. Do you?"

Slater chuckled. "No. When you feel better, we will write down some ideas. Oh, and I called your mom to let her know everything went okay, and she is now a grandma to twin girls."

"Oh, I bet she cried. How is Scottie?"

"Yes, she cried a lot," Slater laughed. "Lorenzo had to come on the phone because she couldn't talk. Scottie is fine. He wants to see the babies. Your mom is coming tomorrow."

The door opened, and an older nurse, probably in her sixties, entered the room. "Hi, I'm nurse Benson, but you can call me

Ruth." She said with a friendly smile. "How are you feeling, Sabela?"

"Sore and tired," I moaned.

"I bet you are, but I bet you can't wait to meet your beautiful daughters." She looked over at Slater and smiled. "Have you decided on names for them yet?"

"No. We were just talking about that."

Ruth walked over to Sabela and checked the machines she was hooked up to. "Well, I'm sure once you are with them, their names will come naturally. Everything looks good here, Sabela. The doctor will be in shortly, and then we will get you over to the NICU ward to see your babies."

I smiled at the thought. "Thank you. When will I be able to hold them and feed them?"

"The doctor will let you know."

Slater walked close to the wheelchair, holding my hand tight as I was being pushed down the hallway to meet our daughters. It was still sinking in that we had twins.

Our world had suddenly changed. Then I thought of Scottie and wished he was here with us to meet his sisters for the first time. He is going to be such a good big brother; I just know it.

After we put on blue sterile gowns and our hands scrubbed, they led us into a room where my eyes were drawn to the two incubators that nursed our babies. I immediately sobbed. "Oh, Slater, they are beautiful."

They wheeled me to the space in between the two cots, and my heart was full. Slater was right. They were tiny and so innocent, but they were perfect in every way. They had very little hair, but what they did seemed to be dark. I looked up at the nurse, Ruth, who had brought us here. "Are they going to be okay? They are so small."

Ruth gave me a reassuring smile that installed my confidence. "They are doing fine. Don't let their size scare you. Once they have gained some strength and weight, you will be able to hold them. I know this is hard, but it will be well worth the wait."

"Thank you." I looked over at Slater, who stood on the other side of one of the nursing cots. Tears streamed down his face. "You are right, Sabela. They are perfect."

Ruth smiled down at our daughters. "Indeed they are. I'm going to be right over there." She pointed to a desk with a computer." If you need me, I'll be right there, okay. You can touch your babies through the sleeved holes on the sides and talk to them."

I looked down, slowly put my hands through the side, and gently rested my palm on one of my baby's chests. Slater did the same with the other. She looked so fragile, and I felt helpless. I wanted to take her in my arms and protect her and have her feel all the love I had to give. "Hi, sweetie. It's mommy. I love you so much," I whispered as Slater echoed my words and introduced himself as daddy to our other daughter.

We looked across at each other as we embraced our new sweet members of our family, and then I began to sing the words softly to the lullaby, *Twinkle Little Star.* Slater soon joined in, and together we sang to our daughters. It was a beautiful moment, and the love I had for these two precious girls seeped from my heart in magnitude. They brought me such joy and hope for my life as a family with Slater, and then it just hit me like Ruth had told me. My heart skipped a beat, and I looked at Slater with bright eyes and smiled. "Hope and Joy. We should name them Hope and Joy."

Slater looked down at his daughters as he stroked one of their tiny hands and grinned. He repeated the names. "Hope and Joy." He looked up and smiled. "The names are perfect. And you don't need to explain why you chose those names. I feel the same way." He looked down again into the cots. "Now, which one is which?"

"This one should be Hope." I stared at the daughter I had my palm on. She was the smallest of the two and had more of a fight to gain her strength.

Slater nodded and smiled at our other daughter. "Hi, Joy."

I whispered their names again. "Hope and Joy. Welcome to our family."

CHAPTER 29

After being in the hospital for almost two weeks, our girls were finally going home. They had released me after three days, and it was so hard to leave the hospital without Hope and Joy. I placed their pictures next to our bed and in every room of the house and sang to the photos every day when I was not with them at the hospital.

Slater and I have been at the hospital every day, bonding with them and telling them about their proud big brother Scottie and their excited grandmother, Charlotte. Three days ago, Slater and I finally got to hold them and feel them in our arms. I never wanted to let them go. Hope was still a little smaller than Joy, and maybe she always will be. For now, it was how we could tell them apart, other than the name tags on their cribs.

My mom and Scottie got to meet them for the first time yesterday. It has been hard for my mom, who met us at the hospital with Lorenzo almost every day, waiting in the lobby for me to send her pictures via phone from their cribs. When I came out to the waiting area yesterday, I told her she could see them and hold them. She broke down and cried as I held her trembling body.

We took Scottie in first and introduced him to his baby sisters. "They look the same." He had said with a creased brow as the two girls laid side by side in the same crib.

Slater had knelt by his side and hugged him. He pointed to Joy on the right. "This is Joy. She is a little bigger than Hope."

Scottie strained his neck. "Yeah, she is, but they are still so small. Was I that small once?"

Slater hesitated before he replied, and I had a gut feeling I knew why. We had talked about it in the past, how he still hurts when he thinks of the years he has missed with Scottie. He was four when he came into our lives. Slater never knew he was a father until then and missed out on his birth and toddler years. Looking at his daughters must make those scars resurface.

Slater gave him the best answer he could. "I'm sure you were that small, buddy."

Now in our truck with Hope and Joy sleeping soundly in their car seats and Scottie on his booster chair in the middle, our family was headed home. While Slater drove, I texted Claire and Jill to give them the good news. Both had yet to meet Hope and Joy since they limited visitors to parents only. Jill didn't bother to text back; instead, she called, and I answered on the first ring.

"You are on your way home?" She screamed into the phone.

I laughed at her excitement. "Yes, we will be there in about ten minutes."

"Oh bummer, and I am at work. Can I come over after? I'm dying to meet them."

"Yes, I invited Claire and Travis too. I can't wait for you to meet them. We need to discuss the wedding too. I have been so out of touch. We have just over three months. I need you to fill me in on where we stand."

"All is good. Claire and I have been working really well together, and your mom has been a lot of help too."

"Oh great! That makes me feel better. I'll see you tonight. I've missed you."

"I've missed you too. Tell Hope and Joy their auntie Jill loves them."

I laughed before ending the call. "Will do."

After Slater had put the truck in park in our driveway, he insisted I go inside, and he would bring the twins in. Still recovering from the c-section, he insisted I do no heavy lifting. For now, Joy and Hope would sleep in cribs next to our beds, but we both agreed it was time to buy a family home. One with a big yard and at least four bedrooms and three bathrooms. "And don't forget a huge garage for me," Slater said.

Settled on the couch, I waited for Slater to bring the babies. Scottie carried the diaper bag, and Slater sat next to me, holding Hope while I cradled Joy in my arms. Scottie sat between us, grinning at his sisters. We were all memorized by the love we felt for these two beautiful girls that have come into our lives.

"I will never get tired of looking, holding, and loving them," I said as I gave Joy a gentle kiss on her forehead.

"Me neither," Slater said. "Why don't I get the bassinets and put them next to you. Scottie can help me get things ready before our friends arrive."

"Sounds good. That was a great idea you had, buying another set of bassinets to keep down here."

"Yeah, it saves going up and downstairs. Jill and Ricky are bringing pizza. Are you good with that?"

"Yes, it sounds good. Claire said she'd bring a salad."

As I relaxed on the couch with Joy and Hope, I glanced over at Slater and Scottie loading the dishwasher together and my heart was full. Everything I ever wanted in my life was right here under this roof. What more could I ever want? We are a family now and in a few months, I will become Slater's wife and take his name with pride. I said my future name out loud and smiled. "Mrs Chester."

Jill arrived first a few hours later and told us Ricky was on his way from work. "Where are my baby girls? Auntie Jill is here."

She screamed with her arms wide open as she raced through the door.

I quickly raised my hands and gave her a hard stare. "Shhh, they are sleeping." My eyes shifted to the bassinets on either side of me.

Jill came to a sudden halt and a quick silence. "Oh shit, I'm sorry. I didn't wake them, did I?" she whispered.

I leaned over Joy's bassinet. "No, thank god. They just went down about five minutes ago."

Jill beamed a big smile as she approached the bassinets and took a seat next to me. "Oh my gosh, they are so beautiful. I want to hold them so badly."

"You will as soon as they wake up in about an hour or so."

Her eyes lit up. "Really!" She held out a bottle of wine that she had been carrying since her arrival. "Can you drink wine now? Ricky is bringing the pizza."

I smiled. "I can and have been. I'm not breastfeeding. I'd have to produce milk all day to feed these two," I chuckled. "Hey, you can feed one if you'd like when they wake up."

Jill's eyes lit up. She glanced around the room and over to the kitchen. "Where are Slater and Scottie? I would love to."

"Upstairs changing."

Jill stood. "Mind if I pour us some wine," she said as she skipped to the kitchen.

Claire and Travis arrived with a salad shortly after Ricky had arrived and just in time to greet Joy and Hope as they were waking up. Tears pooled in Claire's eyes as I handed Hope to her and Slater gave Joy to Jill.

"They are beautiful, Sabela," Claire said as she rocked Hope and gently kissed her forehead. "I'm so happy for you."

I rested my hand on her shoulder. "Thank you. Are you okay? This must be hard for you."

Tears trickled down her cheeks. "I'm okay. A little emotional, maybe, but I know once the children's home opens its doors, we will have our family."

"Oh Claire, yes you will. We are almost there. After the wedding and our honeymoons, the home is our number one priority. You and Travis have done so much already. If it weren't for the wedding, we would be opening soon." I watched as Slater handed Jill a warm bottle of formula, and then Claire made room for them on the couch. Both rocked and hummed tunes as they fed the girls.

"God, this makes me want a baby," Jill giggled.

Ricky quickly turned around, who was playing video games with Scottie on the floor. "What!"

Jill laughed. "Oh, you heard that, didn't you? Don't worry. I was only joking."

"You don't want kids, Jill?" I asked as I took Joy from her and returned her to her bassinet."

"Oh, sure. We want kids someday, but we've not been together that long. We want to have fun with each other for a while."

Claire put Hope in her bassinet and watched her for a few minutes to make sure she didn't wake up. "She's sound asleep," she whispered.

"Good, let's leave the guys here to play with Scottie, and we can go to the kitchen table and discuss the wedding while the girls are sleeping."

"Sounds good," Claire said as we tiptoed away from Hope and Joy."

Jill grabbed some wine from the fridge and three glasses and poured us each a drink before sitting down.

"So, where do we stand with the plans?" I asked, with my notepad open.

"We don't have much left to do," Claire announced. "Invites were sent and are starting to trickle in. The flowers have been ordered. Lorenzo is going to make an amazing multi-colored cake and the restaurant is taking care of everything for the reception."

"I have a band booked and a photographer," Jill interrupted.

"Great," Claire cheered before continuing. "We have a team to set up the decorations for the beach ceremony, including a triple-wide arc and flowers and enough chairs for those invited to that only. The only thing we need to do is pick up our dresses."

"I'm going to have to get mine altered," I said.

"When do you want to do that?" Claire asked.

"Probably Monday when Scottie is in school. My mom can watch the girls."

"Great." Claire looked over at Jill. "Do you want to meet us there on your lunch break?"

"Sure. I can take a longer break if I have to," she giggled. "I can't wait to see our dresses and try them on."

"Me neither," I said and raised my glass. "A toast, ladies."

Claire and Jill matched my glass in the air.

"To marriage. Life doesn't get any better than this."

"To marriage," Jill and Claire echoed.

CHAPTER 30

"You ladies look incredible." Lucy had been our assistant the whole time at the store and had suggested the dipped bridal gowns.

Claire, Jill, and I stood before her, arm in arm, in our dresses, and she was right. They were amazing. The colors were vibrant and cheerful at the base and slowly faded to white at the waistline. I had yellow, Claire had blue, and Jill beamed with pink. "We should call ourselves The Lucky Charm Brides," she joked.

"I like that," Claire agreed.

It was an emotional moment for my mom and Claire's parents, who joined us and wiped away their tears as they stared at their daughters in their wedding gowns. Jill and Claire were able to take theirs home that day, and I picked mine up two weeks later after the alterations were made.

Now two and a half months later, it was the day before our wedding, and I was sitting at the table going over my list, checking to make sure we hadn't missed anything, and I was relieved when I came up blank. As a team, we girls had pulled it off and remained friends. Now, all we had to do was show up and marry the men of our dreams.

I picked up the white wedding ring boxes that sat on the table beside me. Slater and I had picked them out together. Two white gold bands matched the cluster of diamonds on my engagement ring. I held my hand up to the morning sunlight beaming in through the window and admired how it glistened. He promised me a ring after he proposed a few years ago when money was tight, and he had kept that promise by surprising me shortly after Joy and Hope were born.

I was thankful for this quiet time I had this morning. The girls were sleeping upstairs. Slater had taken Scottie out for his favorite pancake breakfast before picking up Scottie's tux from my mom's house, which she picked up last week. He looked so adorable in the white suit and necktie that we had fitted for him, and it matched the men's tux perfectly.

All of us had agreed that we wanted Scottie to be the ring bearer for all three rings. He looked so proud when we asked him. My mom loved the idea and said she would hand him the rings as they were needed.

I sipped on my coffee and thought back to the time I first met Slater on the beach. He stole my heart then, and I gave it to him for life. Suddenly, my phone rang. I glanced at the screen from where it lay on the table. It was Claire, and I quickly took the call.

"She's in her hotel room. She just texted me," Claire said, panting.

"Oh wow. Are you going to call her?"

"I want to, but I would feel so guilty. I still feel bad talking to her before Travis has even met her. God, I hope this crazy idea of surprising him with his mom at the wedding doesn't ruin every-thing. Maybe I should warn him?"

I tried to calm her down. "No, don't do that. You waited this long, and it's your special present to Travis. You are reuniting him with his mom."

Panic was still noticeable in Claire's voice. "I know, but what if he gets pissed and starts yelling? I'll feel awful. It would be all my fault."

I took a deep breath. "Claire, you need to calm down. I honestly think it's a beautiful thing you have done, and I doubt it will upset Travis. He even mentioned to you he had no objections to finding her. He just didn't know where to start. You even told me that."

"Yeah, I know. But what if he has buried resentments towards her for giving him up, and they come pouring out when he is face to face with her? Then what?"

"I think you are overthinking this. Quit thinking about what could go wrong and start thinking about the new relationship that will begin tomorrow between a lost mother and son."

"Yeah, you are right, as always. I'm just so nervous about it. My stomach has been in knots for days. I swear I have lost five pounds. My dress is going to fall off my body."

"It's going to be fine. We will all be there to support you and watch the emotional event." I changed the subject. "Speaking of moms. Jill's parents are arriving this afternoon, and she has invited us to a cocktail hour at the hotel where they are staying. Do you want to go?"

Claire laughed. "Cocktail hour. What shit is that? Don't you mean to drink at the bar?"

I laughed. "It's what her parents call it, I guess. They are staying at that fancy hotel, The Fairmont Grand in Del Mar."

"Oh, I say. How posh. You know I have no fancy clothes. I'm going to stand out like a sore thumb."

"Oh, don't worry about it. Jill said she doesn't want to be alone with her parents. Kind of weird, I thought, so I said I would meet her. It would be us and Ricky's parents who arrived yesterday."

"That is weird. Why doesn't she want to see her parents alone? Did she say what time and how long this is going to take?"

"She said they get in at noon and want to meet for cocktails at two after they've settled in. I told her we could meet for an hour. After all, we are getting married tomorrow."

Claire released a heavy sigh. "Okay, I'll be there in my jeans and a sweatshirt," she laughed.

"We will get to meet Ricky's mom Linda and her boyfriend, Tony. Jill said they are super friendly—down to earth and always talking. She said that she wished her parents were as nice."

"Wow. Does Jill have anything good to say about her parents?"

"Yeah, they send her money every year," I laughed.

After ending the call with Claire, I checked the time and then made a phone call to our hairstylists and makeup artists to confirm they would be here tomorrow at eight, giving us enough time before the ceremony at noon. We had decided that the ladies would dress here and the men would change at Claire's place. My mom would also dress the twins and watch them at the ceremony as they watch on from their white strollers decorated with yellow, pink, and blue flowers.

CHAPTER 31

I arrived at the hotel just as Claire stepped out of her car, and she gave me a big wave. I wound down my window as I pulled alongside her and parked my truck.

"I'm so glad you are here. I didn't want to go in there alone."

I chuckled. "I'm glad to see you too." I glanced at her wardrobe. "You weren't kidding when you said Jeans and a sweatshirt."

Claire opened her arms. "Hey, it's me. I can't pretend to be someone I'm not. I'll meet the wrong people if I do," she joked.

I stepped out of my car and ran my hands down my red dress to smooth out the wrinkles.

"Oh, nice dress Sabela. You, on the other hand, look fantastic."

I smiled. "Thanks. And I admire you for being you. Maybe I should have done the same. I feel overdressed now."

I checked my phone for the time and saw it was five minutes after two and suddenly heard someone call our names behind us.

"Claire. Sabela!"

I turned my head and saw Ricky and Jill hand in hand walking towards us with two older people following along side of them.

I waved and smiled while I waited for them to reach us. "Hey, guys. It's after two. I thought you'd be inside by now."

"Oh hell no. We've been sitting in my car waiting for you two to arrive. There is no way I'm going in there without all of you guys." She turned and held out her hand to the couple standing next to them. "Oh, these are Ricky's folks. "Linda, his mom and her boyfriend Tony."

They held out their hands, which Claire and I shook. "Nice to meet you."

I turned and smiled at Ricky. "You have your mom's eyes."

"Yeah, everyone says that, brilliant blue and thick eyelashes. My sister takes more after our dad."

"Oh, is she here too?" Claire asked.

"Na. Ricky shook his head. She couldn't make it."

"Oh, that's a bummer. I was looking forward to meeting her." Claire replied.

Jill interrupted us. "Okay, guys, let's do this. My mom hates to wait."

"Sounds like someone I know," Claire mumbled under her breath.

Jill rolled her eyes. "I'm nothing like my mom. Don't insult me."

"Wow! Jill. Tell us something good about your mom."

Jill smirked. " She leaves in two days."

Claire and I chatted with Ricky's folks while Jill and Ricky led the way as we walked through the parking lot. I guessed they were in their late fifties, but they looked good. Both had trim bodies and dressed with style. Linda's hair was dark brown, long, straight, and she wore black slacks and a turquoise top. Tony dressed casually in jeans and a light blue shirt. His hair was grey and well-trimmed, which matched his mustache. Linda smiled a lot and talked with her hands. They told us how much they loved Jill and were thrilled that Ricky was finally settling down.

"Jill is great. I told them. We used to work together at the Dentist and have kept in touch since I left."

When we reached the grand main entrance of the hotel, Jill stopped and turned around. She took a deep breath. "Okay, guys, let's get this over with as quickly as possible. I apologize ahead of time for my parents."

"Jill, what kind of thing is that to say?" Claire shrieked.

"Oh, you will understand after we have left. Trust me; you will wish you could leave within five minutes of meeting them."

Claire shrugged her shoulders. "I doubt that. Now come on, let's go inside."

A stiff doorman opened the door. "Good afternoon."

Jill smiled. "Can you tell us where the cocktail lounge is, please?"

"Yes, it's past the front desk on the right."

Jill nodded. "Thank you."

When we entered the dimly lit lounge, soft piano music echoed in my ears, and a lady wearing a large red hat laughing like a hyena caught my attention. She sat with a middle-aged man who whispered something in her ear, and then she waved in our direction. Without having met them yet, I immediately understood Jill's embarrassment.

"Jill darling, mommy is over here."

Jill gave them a forced smile before raising her hand and waving. She turned away and whispered to us. "There she is. The wicked mother."

"Wow, check out her hat," Claire piped.

Jill led the way, and before we reached their table, Jill's mother was already standing with her arms open wide, wearing a fire engine red dress that matched her hat.

"Princess. Mommy has missed you."

"Hi, mom," Jill said with a forced smile. Jill's cheeks were flushed as her mother's arms smothered her. Her face squished against her mother's as she was held tight.

Her mom freed Jill from her arms and tapped her cheek. "Where is my kiss, princess?"

Jill rolled her eyes, leaned in, and gave her mum a peck on the cheek. Her dad, dressed in white slacks and a Hawaiian shirt, wore a huge grin as he stood. "Princess, come give daddy a hug."

Jill moved away from her mom and approached her dad. "Hi, Daddy." He held her in a shoulder hug as she scooched around to face us and reached for Ricky's hand. "This is my fiancé, Ricky. This is my mom and dad, Hank and Pauline."

Ricky nodded and released a nervous cough as he held out his hand to Jill's mother. His cheeks turned a slight shade of red. "Hi Pauline, it's nice to meet you finally."

Pauline laughed and pulled Ricky into her arms. "Oh, stop with all the formal talk. Give me a hug, my soon-to-be son-in-law."

While Ricky was locked in an uncomfortable hug with Jill's mom, Jill introduced us as we took our seats. After finally being released, Ricky shook his head and took a seat next to Jill.

Jill bowed her head as her mom raised her hand and snapped her fingers as she searched the lounge for a waiter or waitress. "Hello," she called to anyone close by. "Can we get some service here?"

"Mom. Stop. One of us can go to the bar and order drinks."

Pauline gave Jill a hard stare. "You or your friends will do no such thing. Do you know how much we are paying for a night to stay here? They can damn well get our drinks for us." She leaned in closer to Jill and stared at her face. "Are you sick, Princess?"

Jill creased her brow. "No, why?"

"Your skin looks so pale. You are hardly wearing any makeup."

"I gave that up a while back. I like being fresh. It's better for my skin."

"Fresh. What kind of word is that? You look half dead. You look so much better with your bright pink lipstick and eyes painted with that thick mascara. I'm not sure if I like you this way." Pauline patted her cheeks and fluttered her heavy painted eyes. "Look at me. Mommy still looks good. And it's because I take care of myself."

Jill glanced our way, where we all sat in silence, and rolled her eyes. "My skin feels much better. It's able to breathe, mom. I prefer this look."

"I see you have also gained a few pounds," her mother snarled. "You need to take better care of yourself if you want to look as good as me when you reach my age."

Suddenly Jill snapped. "Mom, why do you always have to criticize me? I've not seen you in god knows how many years, and all you can do is find fault with me."

"Well, I see your mouth hasn't changed. I'm looking out for you, princess. There is a difference, you know, and don't talk to your mommy in that way." She looked over at her husband. "Hank, are you going to let your daughter talk to her mother that way?"

Jill's dad raised his hand. "Leave me out of this. You, two always bicker at each other when you get together."

A waiter approached our table.

"About time." Pauline snarled. "Do you know how long we have been waiting? I thought this was a five-star hotel with 5-star service."

"Mom, be quiet," Jill hissed as she cowered her head.

"I'm sorry, ma'am, we have been quite busy, but I'd be happy to take your drink order now."

Pauline looked across at Claire and me. "So are these the two ladies that are sharing your wedding day, and why is that? We send you plenty of money every year. You should be able to afford your own wedding."

Jill turned to her mom and narrowed her eyes. "Mom, these are my best friends, and we wanted to share our special day together. This has nothing to do with money."

"Yes, Jill and I used to work together," I added.

"Oh, did you work at that dentist's place, too? I guess you are smarter than my daughter. She apparently is still working there."

I was lost for words. I now understood Jill's embarrassment, and her dad silently nodded as his wife continued to ridicule their daughter.

"It's a great place to work," Claire said, trying to give Jill some support. "I used to work there too."

"Well, it can't be that great if you left also."

Pauline changed the subject and narrowed her eyes at Ricky. "So, what do you do for a living?"

Ricky shifted in his seat and took Jill's hand. "I'm in construction, ma'am."

"A builder," Pauline said in a flat tone. "So tell me, will your salary be enough to support our daughter?"

"Mom. What kind of question is that?"

"Well, sweetheart. You don't expect your father and me to keep sending you checks after you are married, do you? It will be Ricky's job to take care of you. I'm just making sure he is up for the job. After all, you are high maintenance, darling. I should know. I'm your mommy, and I raised you that way."

Jill glared at her mother and snarled. "You didn't raise me; my nannies raised me. Who changed every six months, by the way, because they couldn't stand you. You and daddy were too busy flying around the world. And to answer your question, Ricky and I will be fine. We don't need your money."

"You know damn well your father and I were not around because we were working hard to make good money so we could give you the life you have had. Your father is an internationally well-established lawyer, and he didn't get there by sitting at home."

"You were busy partying and drinking cocktails with your rich friends." Jill stood and shook her head vigorously. "I'm done here. I'm sick of your insults and you demeaning me. Never have you acted like a mother to me. Ha! You've never been around, so how could you."

Pauline scanned the lounge, afraid her image was being scarred by her daughter's outburst, and waved her hand at Jill. "Jill, will you sit down? People are staring at us."

"No, I won't sit down. That's all you care about is your own image." She gave her dad a hard stare. "And you, dad. You don't even defend me. You just sit there with that stupid smirk on your face while mom insults me."

"Hey, Princess. I told you not to bring me into this. Your mother doesn't mean anything by it. She's always been this way. It's her way of showing she cares."

Pauline smiled at her husband. "Thank you, sweetheart. I only wish our daughter would see it that way instead of making a spectacle of herself and embarrassing all of us."

"Mom! Will you stop! You can't even open your mouth without dropping an insult. I'm sick of it. I'm getting married tomorrow, and you have not even asked anything about the wedding or how happy you are for Ricky and me."

Pauline gritted her teeth when she spoke. "Your father and I traveled halfway across the world to be here. Isn't that enough? We spent thousands on plane tickets and a hotel room that is supposed to be the best in the area. They will be hearing from me, might I add." She looked over her shoulder at the bar. "Where are our damn drinks?"

"There you go again. It's all about money," Jill snapped. "You have to remind everyone how much money you put out, and we should all bow to you and be at your mercy. God, you are so self-centered," Jill cracked a sarcastic laugh. "Wow! Thank god I changed. I used to be just like you." Jill shook her head and bit her lip. "I never realized that until now. What a terrifying thought. I actually saved myself without knowing it."

Pauline furrowed her brow. "What are you talking about? Saved yourself? You are making no sense. What has happened to you?"

Jill released another sarcastic laugh. "What has happened to me? I broke away from the mold and became my own person. Give me a call when you want to acknowledge that and act like a mom who is proud of her daughter. Until then, I have a wedding to get ready for."

Jill looked at the rest of us, who had remained silent. "Are you guys ready? We are done here."

Ricky stood first and nodded to Jill's father. "It was a pleasure meeting you."

Hank mirrored his nod. "Likewise."

Ricky's mom and Tony stood next. "Okay then. We will see you tomorrow at the wedding."

"That's it. After you insulted your father and me, you are leaving?"

"How does it feel, mom? Come on, Claire and Sabela, there is nothing more to say here."

Claire and I gave each other a puzzled look, shrugged our shoulders, and stood. "Nice to meet both of you," I said as I held out my hand.

Pauline waved off my hand and stared down at Jill. "How dare you embarrass me like this. I am your mother."

Jill turned before she walked away. "And I am your daughter. But I never felt like it. Goodbye, mother."

In silence, we all followed Jill's lead as she marched out of the lounge. Once outside, Jill folded into Ricky's arms and cried.

"I'm so sorry that you guys had to see that. She is such a witch. I have never stood up to her like that before." And then she threw back her head and laughed. "God, it felt friggin awesome."

Ricky laughed with her. "I was really proud of you. I can't believe how she was talking to you."

"And that was her being nice. She held back a lot. You didn't see the worst of it. Again I'm sorry, everyone."

"Hey, it's okay. Don't apologize," I said, resting my hand on her shoulder. "Are you going to be okay?"

Still wrapped in Ricky's arms, Jill nodded. "Yeah, I'll be fine. It was a long time coming. I couldn't take it anymore."

"Do you think they will come to the wedding tomorrow?" Claire asked.

Jill released a heavy sigh. "Knowing my wicked mother. No. She's probably already checking out of the hotel and looking for the next available flight back to their exotic villa. For the first time, her daughter stood up to her, and she had no idea how to handle that, except to run away and ignore it."

I gave her a caring smile. "I'm sorry, Jill."

"It's fine. She'd just ruin the wedding anyway," she smiled, wiping the last of her tears away. "I have what I want right here. Good friends and an amazing man."

Ricky leaned in and gave her a long, sweet kiss on the lips. "I love you, baby."

"I love you too. Now come on, let's go home. We are getting married tomorrow."

The sound of one of the twins crying woke me from my deep sleep. I turned and looked at the clock on the nightstand. It was only four in the morning, but then I remembered I was getting married today. Nothing was going to ruin this day.

I looked down at Slater, who was sleeping peacefully, and smiled. In a few hours, he will be my husband. I got goosebumps just thinking about it and rubbed my arms before kissing Slater softly on his forehead. "I love you," I whispered before crawling out of bed and wrapping my body in my bathrobe.

Joy was the one that was crying and soon woke her sister Hope. "Sssh baby. I'll be right back with a bottle for both of you."

By the time I returned to our bedroom, Slater was awake and rocking Joy in his arms. "Hey, I'm sorry they woke you," I whispered as I picked up Hope and gave her a bottle, and handed the other one to Slater. In seconds the room fell silent, and Slater and I released heavy sighs.

"God, I know I say this every time I hold one of them, but they are so perfect in every way." He said as he looked down at Joy cradled in his arms.

"They are. We do good work," I laughed.

Within fifteen minutes, the girls were sound asleep and back in their bassinets. Slater was already under the covers and sat up as he patted the empty space next to him.

"Come back to bed. I want to hold you in my arms one last time as an unwed woman."

"Hmmm, I love you so much," I said with eyes closed and my arms draped over his chest. I giggled and slid my body under the covers and pressed it firmly against his.

Slater pulled me in and gave my body a tight squeeze. "I love you too. If the twins weren't in here, I'd be all over you."

I looked up and gave him a flirty smile. "Wanna take a shower?"

Slater quickly pulled back the covers and took my hand. "You don't have to ask me twice."

Behind the closed doors of the bathroom, we ran the shower full blast to drown out sounds of passion and kissed with hunger as we closed the shower door behind us, making sure it clicked. Slater didn't waste a second to take me in his arms and kiss me hard as he kneaded his hands all over my now wet body. His touch was full of lust and desire. It has been a while since we've had sex, and neither one of us was holding back.

I raved over Slater's muscular, tanned body, caressing every inch as he kissed my soft skin and tasted it with his tongue. I moaned when he took my breasts into his mouth and blew his hot breath over my nipples. It wasn't long before he was inside me. I faced the slate-tiled wall and let out a loud, satisfying moan when I felt all of him.

"Oh my god, I have missed this feeling," Slater moaned as he thrust his pelvis, pushing himself deeper inside of me. "You feel so damn good," he cried before thrusting again. This time, harder, and each thrust after had more force than the one before.

"Don't stop," I cried as I pressed my palms firmly against the shower wall. "You are going to make me come."

Slater kept thrusting his hips, picking up speed. I matched his rhythm until we both couldn't hold back anymore, and with one last hard push, we came. Slater quickly leaned in, and I turned my head to meet his lips and kissed him passionately to silence our orgasmic screams. Our chests heaved, and our breaths were loud.

"The next time we do this, you will be a married woman." Slater panted between breaths. "Do you know how sexy that sounds?"

I giggled and slowly turned around and leaned against the cool tile. It felt good. "And I like the idea of a married man making love to me," I added. We kissed again. Slater pushed my body against the wall and pressed his chest hard against mine as he explored my mouth with his tongue. "I don't want to stop. Let's skip the wedding and hide in here all day."

I broke our kiss and slapped his chest. "Slater! As tempting as that sounds, I want to be your wife. And today is that day."

When we returned to the bedroom, we grabbed our bathrobes and tiptoed out of the room to not wake the twins.

Over coffee, I sat on Slater's lap with my arm hooked around his neck and his around my waist.

"So what time do Scottie and I have to be out of here?"

"The make-up artists and hairdressers will be here at eight. The limo will be here at eleven, and there will be a limo for you guys at Claire's place at the same time. The beach ceremony is at noon, and the reception at the restaurant starts at two. I don't know how many times I have told you all this." I laughed.

"I don't know how you keep track of everything."

"It's not been easy. But mom has been a huge help." I glanced at the clock on the kitchen wall. "Okay, you have an hour and a half to grab all of yours and Scottie's things and be out of here before people show up," I said as I left his lap and stood.

Slater impressed me by leaving fifteen minutes before the hour of eight. After another feeding, the twins were sound asleep, and I had just enough time to text mom, Claire, and Jill to make sure they were not running late. They were not. In fact, my mom knocked at the door within two minutes of me texting her.

I opened the door and looked over her shoulder. "Where's Lorenzo?"

"He can't come here. This is for the brides only. He is meeting us on the beach."

Mom scanned the front room. "Where are my baby girls?"

"They just went down and are sleeping upstairs. They are officially yours now for the rest of the day. You are in charge." I told her with a huge smile.

Mom clapped her hands. "Don't you worry."

"Their dresses are laid out on our bed, and you brought all the decorations for the strollers, right?"

My mom rolled her eyes. "Yes, I have them in my car and my dress too."

By eight-thirty, everyone had arrived. After introductions and cheers of excitement from my best friends and more hugs than needed, the three make-up artists and three hairdressers began to set up their spaces to perform their magic on us.

"When are you leaving for Vegas?" I asked Jill, who sat on a stool in front of a mirror with her hair bound in rollers.

"Tomorrow. Our flight leaves at eleven in the morning.

Claire sat across the room, sitting in front of a mirror while her hair was being worked on. "Whose idea was it to go to Vegas for your honeymoon?"

"Both of ours. We love Vegas, and it was a no-brainer." She turned and looked at Claire. "What about you and Travis? You said something about camping in Yosemite. Are you still doing that?" Jill creased her brow. "Sleeping on the ground with bugs seems kinda weird for a honeymoon if you ask me."

"Jill. They like camping." I hollered from across the room as the hairdresser teased my hair.

"Yes, we are still going camping, but we are waiting until next spring, which is my favorite time of year. Everything is new and fresh and all the plants and trees are blooming. It will also give Travis more time to gain more strength and be almost back to normal. Camping is perfect for us, Jill. We love it, and it's been ages since we have been. We plan on going on lots of hikes, kayaking on the lakes, and having a cozy campfire every night. Just me, Travis, and nature. Oh, and Tilly," she added. "It can't get any better than that."

Jill curled her lip. "Not for me, thanks. No way. That's a long time to wait, though, to go on your honeymoon."

"Not for us. We still need to finalize things at the foster home, and Travis needs an all-clear from his doctors. The more time we let go by, the better chances he has of no objection from his doctor," Claire replied.

"So when is the children's home going to be open?" Jill asked.

"Well, the way Travis and Claire are going. Our final permit will be issued around February of next year. We plan on taking our first child when they return from Yosemite. Claire and Travis will have everything arranged before they leave." I turned and looked at Claire. "Right Claire?"

Claire nodded. "Yes. I can't believe that we will be taking children in and raising them as our own."

Jill had another question. "What about the kids that come in and then get adopted out. Won't that be hard on you guys?"

Claire clasped her hands together and bowed her head. It was something I had not thought about, but it was obvious Claire had.

"Travis and I have talked about that and thought really hard about it. For some time, we questioned if we wanted to pursue the business, but Travis and I finally came to terms with what we are doing is more for the children. Making sure they get a chance in life and a good start. That's what matters. We are the beginning of that new start; the next step is a permanent home. A sense of belonging with a family that will love them. We are that bridge that will make it happen." She gave Jill and me each a smile. "And we may, if we feel we have a strong bond with a child or two, adopt them permanently."

"Oh, that would be brilliant, Claire," I cried.

"What about you and Slater? When do you leave for Hawaii?" Claire asked.

"We are going to wait awhile, too. We want to wait until Joy and Hope are a little older. Mom will be watching them. Slater suggested next summer, and I agreed."

"I think that's a good idea," Claire said with a nod.

A few hours later, we brought tears to my mom's eyes as she stood at the bottom of the stairs. The decked-out white strollers, decorated with pink, yellow, and blue flowers, stood before her. The twins, dressed in their matching white lace dresses dipped dyed yellow to match my dress, slept peacefully inside.

Mom was dressed in a beautiful pastel yellow dress and held her hands up to her mouth as she gasped at my two best friends and me as we walked slowly down the stairs in our wedding dresses.

"Oh my goodness. You all look so beautiful," my mom cried.

Jill reached the bottom of the stairs first and did a twirl. "We do, don't we." She giggled as she admired her pink dip-dyed dress in the full-length mirror.

"Your dresses are beautiful, and I love the matching colored flowers in your hair."

I reached my mom and embraced her. "Thanks, mom. And Hope and Joy look amazing. You did a great job."

"I just fed them. They should sleep for a while."

Claire turned to us and smiled. Her body trembled.

I took her hand. "Claire, are you okay?"

"Yes. I'll be fine. I can't stop thinking about Travis's mom. She should be texting me soon. Am I doing the right thing by not telling Travis?"

Jill released a cocky laugh. "Well, it's a little late to be asking that. An hour before the big surprise is supposed to happen."

I scolded Jill. "Jill, you are not helping." She then turned to talk to Claire. "Everything is going to be okay. Is she meeting him before or after we get married?"

"I don't know. If it happens before, it might ruin everything for Travis. And besides, we won't see our men until we are at the big arch. What am I supposed to do? Drag Travis away and tell everybody to hold on a minute while I take him to meet his mom, seconds before he is supposed to say I do."

Suddenly there was a knock at the door. "That's the limo. Let's talk about this on the way." I said as I took Claire's hand. A minute later, her phone got a text message. Claire glanced at the screen. Her eyes widened.

"That's her. What should I tell her?"

CHAPTER 33

My eyes raced around the front room toward the kitchen, checking to see if I had forgotten anything.

"Are the car seats in your car, mom?"

"Yes, one of the nice hairdresser ladies helped me before she left."

Being careful not to wake the twins, I helped my mom load them in her car and was thankful they didn't stir as I clipped the seatbelts in place. "You have plenty of formula?" I asked, giving each girl a gentle kiss on their foreheads.

"Quit worrying. I have everything I need." She held up the white diaper bag I had packed last night and leaned in to give me a peck on the cheek. "You look beautiful, Sabela. I wish your dad could see you."

"He can, mom. Now don't make me cry. My makeup will get ruined. I'll see you in the parking lot at the beach. Claire's Mom and dad will be there to help you with the twins."

I waited as my mom got in her car. She waved before pulling out of the driveway. I waved back as she disappeared down the street and then made a dash for the white limo. The door was wide open. Claire and Jill waved me in.

"Come on, Sabela. We have to go," Jill yelled from inside the limo.

"Coming," I yelled back.

I stepped in and gasped. "Wow, this is fancy." I ran my hands over the plush cream velvet seats and scooted my feet across the thick pile of light pink carpet.

"Did you notice the three shades of flowers on the hood? Pink, yellow and blue," Claire said with a huge grin.

"I did. This thing is huge. I've never been in a limo before," I confessed."

"Me neither," Claire added.

"I have, in Vegas. But it wasn't this fancy, and it didn't have the pink neon lights in the ceiling. I love those." She said with bright eyes. "And look at all this booze," she added, while holding up a bottle of chilled champagne. "Who wants some bubbly?"

"I do," Claire said. "I need something to calm my nerves, and I need to text Caroline back. What am I going to tell her?"

Jill handed me a glass of champagne, and I took a large gulp. The bubbles traveled up my nose and made me laugh. "That tickles my nose." I looked over at Claire, who sat across from me, and noticed her glass was already empty. Jill poured her another one.

"Okay, Claire. Well, it's obvious Travis can't meet his mom before we are married. You were right when you said we can't pull him away a few minutes before the ceremony begins." I had an idea. "What about at the reception? She can wait for us there."

Claire shook her head. "I can't do that to her. She traveled all this way to watch her son get married."

I bit my lip and thought some more. "Jill, do you have any ideas?"

"Nope."

"Thanks, you're a lot of help," Claire said with an edge.

"How about we just don't say anything until after we are married? I suggested.

"You mean don't talk to her at all?" Claire said with a creased brow.

I shrugged my shoulders. "Well, I can't think of any other way. We don't want to risk ruining the wedding for Travis, in case he happens to get upset." I saw Claire's worried look. "Which I doubt he will be," I quickly added.

"But Travis is going to wonder who she is. He may try to talk to her while our men are waiting for us to arrive. I don't know if I want to take that chance." Claire bit her lip. "He's going to know everyone there, my parents, maybe Jill's parents, your mom, Ricky's mom and Tony, Sadie, and the kids. Caroline will be the only stranger."

"Shit! Damn, you didn't think this all the way through, did you?" I said, while racking my brain for another idea.

"Sorry, no, I didn't."

"Why can't she just be late?" Jill casually suggested, while sipping on her second glass of champagne.

Claire gave her a puzzled look. "What? She can't be late. How will that solve things? And besides, she'll miss the wedding."

"Not necessarily," Jill said with a smirk.

"Jill, we are not following you?" I said, feeling just as confused as Claire.

Jill leaned back and raised her hands. "Look, when it's our time to walk across the beach to the arch, our guys will already be there waiting for us, right?"

"Yes, that's right," I confirmed.

"And all the guests will be there?" Jill asked.

"Yes. only family members and Sadie have been invited to the actual wedding."

Jill took a sip of her drink while Claire and I waited patiently for her to tell us her plan.

"Well, what if Travis's mom walks down a few minutes after us and arrives when we are standing next to our men moments before we get started? Travis may wonder who she is, but he can't leave and ask her minutes before he is about to get married. And if he tries, Claire will be there to stop him."

I gave Jill a huge smile. "That's brilliant!"

Claire matched my smile. "Jill, I agree. It's a great idea. Thank you."

Jill gave us a smug smile. "You are welcome."

Okay, text Caroline and tell her to meet us in the parking lot of the Fisherman's Grill restaurant."

Claire grabbed her phone from the seat next to her and began tapping the screen at great speed.

A few minutes later, after back and forth texting, she looked up and smiled. "Okay, she will be there. She is twenty minutes away in a cab."

"Tell her to stay in the cab until we get there. The men need to walk down to the beach before she gets out."

"I'm on it," Claire said, working her fingers across the screen. "God, I hope we can pull this off," she said, after sending the final text.

CHAPTER 34

"There she is!" Claire hollered while pointing to a yellow cab on the other side of the parking lot. "I don't think it's right to talk to her again. I feel bad enough that I have spoken to her once already. It should be Travis that speaks to her next."

"Tell her to wait in the car and come down to the beach five minutes after we have left."

Claire nodded. "Will do."

I looked over at Jill, who smacked her lips after finishing her champagne in one gulp.

I laughed. "Are we a little nervous?"

"Maybe I'm a bit nervous." Jill looked out of the window. "Here comes your dad Claire."

Claire looked up from her phone. "Okay, Caroline is heading down in five minutes."

Being closest to the door, I pushed it open and smiled at Claire's dad as he approached the limo. He took my hand as I stepped out. "Thank you."

While waiting for Jill and Claire to exit the car, I scanned the parking lot and smoothed out my dress.

"You look beautiful, Sabela," Jeffery said as he waited for Claire to exit the limo.

"Thank you." I turned and looked at Jill, who was teasing her hair with her hands. "I don't see your dad, Jill."

Jill looked around from where we stood. "I'm not surprised. They are probably halfway across the Atlantic. Screw them!"

"I'm sorry, Jill." I looked over at Claire, who was in the middle of an embrace with her dad. "Well, it looks like you are the only one walking down with their dad." I patted my heart. "I have my dad right here. He will be with me."

Claire freed herself from her dad's hold. "Scottie has all the rings, right?"

"Yes. My mom will be helping him. She texted me and said your mom and Ricky's mom will take care of Joy and Hope while the ceremony is taking place."

I gave my best friends a huge smile. "Well, ladies, are we ready to get married?"

"You betcha. I miss Ricky. I've not seen him since this morning." Jill said while adjusting some of the flowers in her bouquet.

"Well, in about thirty minutes, you will be able to call him your husband," Claire said as she locked arms with her dad.

I reached down and pulled off my shoe. "Almost forgot, barefoot remember."

In haste, we all stripped our feet of our shoes and tossed them in the back of the limo.

When we reached the beach, everyone stood. I looked over at the white arch decorated with pink, yellow, white, and blue flowers. I saw Slater standing tall, with his hands together in front of him. He smiled, and I smiled back. He looked handsome in his white tuxedo, his hair brushed back, and a yellow rose in his lapel. Scottie stood beside him in a matching tuxedo and rose. Next to him stood my mom, holding the ring cushion with all of our rings. We choose not to have any music. The natural sound of the waves crashing against the shore and the gentle breeze whispering through our hair was perfect.

Before we continued to walk, Jill stopped us and took mine and Claire's hand. "I love you guys. You are my family now. I will never forgive my mom and dad for not being here."

I squeezed Jill's hand. "We will always be family. After all, the twins love their auntie, Jill."

Claire gave Jill a loving smile. "She's right. We love you, Jill. Now come on, our men are waiting for us."

We all took our places next to our future husbands.

Slater smiled. "Hi. You look gorgeous," he whispered.

"So do you," I whispered back.

I glanced at the small crowd of family and saw the tears pooled in my mom's eyes. "I love you, mom," I said, blowing her a kiss.

A few minutes later, I noticed all heads turning in the direction we had just come from and turned my head. A middle-aged woman with dark brown hair, dressed in a blue floral dress, was walking our way. I immediately knew who it was. It was Travis's mom. She looked nervous, walking by herself, and I felt sad for her.

"Is that who I think it is?" Slater whispered in my ear.

"Yes. Don't say anything."

"I won't."

I looked over at Claire, who sneaked me a nervous smile. Her hand wrapped in Travis's tightly. As Caroline neared the crowd, I eased her noticeable nerves with a friendly smile. She nodded and kept a few feet away from the rest of us.

"Who is that?" Travis asked Claire.

"Shh, here is the minister. I'll tell you after."

Travis creased his brow. "You know her?"

Claire silenced him. "Hush, we are getting started."

The minister welcomed our families, watching on before asking each of us to say our vows. Tears rolled down my cheeks as I held

Slater's hands and looked into his eyes. I was so nervous, but in a good way, and not once did I take my eyes off Slater. After declaring my love for him, I smiled when I said the final words. "I do."

Scottie and my mom walked up to each of us and handed us the rings, and at the same time, Claire and Travis placed their rings on each other's fingers. Jill and Ricky did theirs, and Slater and I did ours.

The minister smiled. "I now pronounce you man and wife. You may kiss the bride."

Cheers erupted around us as we folded into our husband's arms and kissed each other for the first time as husband and wife. After breaking away from Slater with my heart full and tears of joy gushing down my face, I embraced Claire and Travis, and within seconds Ricky and Jill joined us for a group hug.

"Congratulations, guys. We did it," Slater yelled at the top of his voice.

Cheers and congratulations continued for the next few minutes, and then I saw Claire taking Travis's hand and leading him over to Caroline. I pulled away from my mom's embrace. "Mom, I'll be right back." I quickly scurried over to Slater, who was shaking Ricky's hand. I tapped him on the shoulder. "Look over there."

Slater looked up and followed my eyes. "Oh shit. Claire's taking him to meet Caroline."

I took Slater's hand. "Let's get a little closer so we can hear what is being said and give support if needed."

"Good idea."

I watched and pinned my ears a few feet away. Caroline stood with her hands clasped together and wearing a nervous smile as Claire and Travis approached her. Slater and I avoided eye contact with them and held our breath.

Claire spoke first. "Travis, this is someone I would like you to meet."

Travis held out his hand. "Hi, I don't think I know you. Are you a relative of someone here?"

Claire answered for her. "As a matter of fact, she is."

"Oh really, who?"

I took in a deep breath, anticipating Claire's reply, and saw Slater did the same. "This is intense," he whispered.

"Shh," I quickly uttered back.

Claire looked at Travis and smiled. She took his hand. "Travis, this is your mom, Caroline Trent. I found her and wanted to surprise you on our wedding day. It is my gift to you. You reunited me with my parents, and I wanted to do the same for you."

There was silence. My nerves were on edge. "Someone say something," I muttered under my breath.

Caroline spoke next. "Hello, Travis. I've waited so long to meet you."

The shock Travis was feeling couldn't go unnoticed. His jaw dropped, and his eyes were on fire. He stood back and raised a hand to his brow, and gave Caroline a puzzled look. "You are my mom?"

Caroline nodded. "I am. Claire found me through an agency."

Travis turned and looked at Claire. His brow still creased, and then I noticed he let go of her hand. Fear swept over her face.

"You did this, Claire? You found my mom?"

Claire bit her lip, and her chest heaved before she spoke. "I did, Travis. You are not mad, are you?"

Travis ignored Claire's question and looked at Caroline again. "You are my mom? Wow. I don't know what to say. I'm in shock." He turned and looked at Claire again. "I can't believe you did this."

Claire reached for Travis's hand, and I was pleased to see he didn't pull away. "Please tell me you're not mad."

When Travis shook his head, I suddenly felt at ease.

"No, no, sweetheart. I'm just stunned. I just got married and still can't believe you are my wife, and now I'm meeting my mom for the first time. Wow! It's a lot to take in."

Claire raised her hands to her chest. "Oh, thank god."

She turned to Caroline, who was now crying tears of joy. "Why don't you give your son a hug."

"Can I?" she asked in a soft voice with her arms open.

Tears flooded my eyes as I watched Travis embrace his mom. Claire watched on as she wiped the endless tears that she was experiencing, and when I looked over at Slater, I saw he was wiping tears away too.

"This is beautiful to watch," I said as I leaned my head on Slater's shoulder.

"It sure is," Slater said before kissing me on the lips.

With his arm around his mom and another arm around Claire, he yelled at the crowd. "Hey, everyone! I want you to meet my mom." He turned to Claire and kissed her passionately on the lips. "Thank you, Claire, for giving me the greatest gift ever."

CHAPTER 35

After giving Travis and Claire a joyous hug and introducing myself to Caroline, it relieved me that Claire's surprise gift was a huge success. I could tell that Caroline was relieved too. I could only imagine the anxieties she must have been feeling. Whatever signs of nervousness she was experiencing had completely disappeared. She gave her son, Travis, thirty years' worth of hugs, and the love that seeped from her eyes couldn't be denied. Like his mom's, Travis's eyes were bright, and his smile was big, and the loving look he gave Claire brought tears to my eyes. A piece of the puzzle from Travis's past had been found and brought home.

I could see the resemblance between Caroline and Travis. He had her brown eyes and rounded chin, and their smiles were the same too.

"I'm so happy for you both," I said while Travis held on to the two women in his life. "This was a wonderful thing you did, Claire," I told her and squeezed her hand.

"It really was, honey." Travis agreed. He turned and looked at his mom. "I hope you are going to be here for a while. I have so many questions for you."

"I'm here for a week. I want to get to know everything about you and all the things I have missed." Tears filled her eyes. "I'm so sorry, Travis. I never wanted to give you up, but I had no choice. I was forced to."

Travis quickly silenced her. He knew she was just a child herself when she had him. "It's okay, mom," he paused and chuckled. "Wow! It feels weird and, at the same time, good to call someone mom. Is it okay if I call you mom?" he asked Caroline.

"Yes, I would love it, son," she said with a soft smile.

Travis continued to finish what he was saying. "Please don't feel bad about giving me up. I know your parents made you. The important thing is, and thanks to my wife, we have each other now."

After Travis and Claire made the rounds and introduced Caroline to everyone, I scanned the beach and saw my mom and Ricky's mom feeding the twins. And Slater and Scottie were playing tag by the waves. Jill And Ricky were embraced in a long passionate kiss, and Lorenzo was in a deep conversation with Claire's parents. I turned to Claire.

"Okay, Mrs. Trent, the photographer, has all the pictures he needs. Are we ready to head up to the reception? When we do, everyone else will follow. The rest of the guests should already be gathering in the banquet room."

"Yes. Let's grab our husbands and all walk in together."

I smiled. "I like that." I looked over at Jill and Ricky again and saw they were still embraced in a kiss. "I may have a problem breaking up those two." I laughed.

Suddenly, I was deafened by Claire's voice. "Hey, Jill! Hey Ricky, give it a rest. Let's go!"

Jill and Ricky quickly broke apart and looked our way.

"That worked." Claire said triumphantly. "Come on; we are

heading up to the restaurant." She shouted while waving at them to join us.

"Who needs a foghorn when we have you." I joked and then turned to look where I last saw Slater and Scottie. "Here comes Slater too. He must have also heard you."

A few minutes later, we were all in the arms of our new husbands. After giving my baby girls and Scottie a smooch, we instructed everyone to head up to the restaurant and we would follow in ten minutes.

I turned and smiled at my two best friends, Claire and Jill. "I'm so happy we shared this special day together. It is something Slater and I will treasure for the rest of our lives."

Everyone agreed and nodded their heads. "I wouldn't want to have gotten married any other way," Claire replied.

Travis squeezed her. "Me neither, babe." To be reunited with my mom makes it even more special."

"Thank you, guys. I love you all so much." Jill squealed while she bounced on her heels, wrapped in Ricky's arms.

Slater took my hand and spoke next. He smiled at Ricky and Travis. "Guys, we have just married our best friends, and I think I speak for all of us when I say we couldn't be happier. They are everything to us. Without them, we would have nothing."

Jill leaned into Ricky and rested her head on his shoulder. "Aww, that is the sweetest thing."

"Well said, man." Travis agreed with a nod.

"So, are we ready to kick up some heels, drink some fine wine, and party with friends for the rest of the day and night?" Slater said with a brilliant smile.

"You betcha!" Jill yelled. I need a beer.

hen all six of us entered the large banquet room, the party was already in full swing. Prince blasted through the speakers, and a large crowd had gathered. I scanned the room and saw many people I didn't recognize, but there were six of us that had invited friends. There were bound to be some I didn't know.

The room looked beautiful with its pink, yellow and blue table-cloths and flower arrangements in the same color. I looked across the room at the top table where we would be sitting and saw that it had three different colored tablecloths. It looked fantastic with the matching flowers, and to the left of the table was the cake table with the beautiful 3 tier multi-colored cake Lorenzo had made, and on each tier sat a plastic bride and groom. It was perfect.

"Here they are!" someone shouted from the crowd. In one swift movement, all heads turned towards us and cheered as we walked through the room, holding our spouse's hands. We nodded and hugged the ones we knew and took our seats at the top table.

Champagne was poured after the food was served, and toasts

and speeches were given. Me, Claire and Jill joined our husbands on the dance floor for the first dance while our friends and parents looked on. It was a magical moment that would stay with me forever.

As the afternoon turned to evening, the party was in full swing. My mom and Lorenzo would be leaving in about an hour to take the twins and Scottie back to her place for the night. I was amazed at how good the girls had been all day. I looked across the room and saw Scottie had made some new friends with other kids, and Slater was joking with Travis nearby.

Jill and Ricky were doing the salsa on the dance floor in the middle of a cheering crowd, and Claire had just left me to check on her mom and dad. Finally, I was able to take a breather and be alone for a few minutes and began heading back to my seat when I felt a tap on my shoulder and a familiar voice.

"It's been a long time, Sabela. I'm disappointed that you didn't wait for me."

I froze as my heart pounded, remaining silent.

I felt the tap again. "Sabela. Don't be rude. Aren't you at least going to say hello?"

Chills swarmed my body. I recognized the creepy voice but wanted to be wrong.

"Turn around, Sabela. Let me look at you."

A huge lump wedged in my throat. I couldn't move. My body shook, and my heart hammered against my chest. "Please be wrong," I said over and over again in my head, but I wasn't.

Even though he was wearing a black baseball hat that almost covered his eyes and an untrimmed beard, there was no denying that it was Davin. The man that tried to rape me and raped others. Fear swept through me as I struggled to say his name. My voice trembled when I spoke. "Davin. What are you doing here? I thought you were in jail."

"Well, you thought wrong, pretty lady. When I heard you were getting hitched, I busted out of that damn place, and I'm here to take back what's mine," he hissed.

I tried to hide the fear I felt when I spoke, but knew I had failed. "You heard? Who told you?" I didn't want to wait for an answer and quickly turned to run away. I needed to find Slater and spoke in a harsh whisper, "Davin, you have to leave. I'm married. Please go."

With a sharp tug, Davin grabbed my arm and spun me around, and hollered. "Don't you walk away from me bitch!"

Suddenly, the crowd went silent, and the music stopped. All eyes were upon us. Davin pulled me in and wrapped his arm around my neck as I struggled to break away. "Davin, let me go," I begged between coughs.

"Shut up," he screamed with eyes that resembled the devil.

I was unable to move as Davin had a chokehold around my neck and looked at the horrified crowd.

I heard a woman scream, "Davin, no!"

Davin screamed back. "Shut up, mom! Sabela is leaving with me, and no one is going to stop me."

I couldn't turn my head or move my body. As hard as I tried to break away, Davin would push or squeeze me harder.

I tried to speak and beg Davin to let me go but failed. The pressure on my neck was too much.

I heard Slater's voice. He tried to speak in a calm voice, but I detected his fear. "Davin, let her go. Let's talk about this."

Davin tugged me, and my feet slid on the floor as he began to drag me to where I could only guess was the exit. "There's nothing to talk about. Leave us alone. Sabela belongs to me. I told you that a long time ago, but you didn't listen."

I heard Claire's mom scream again. "Davin, Please! Stop this. Let her go."

Davin heaved his chest. Rage spilled from his mouth when he spoke. "I told you to stay out of this, mom."

Slater spoke again, only this time he sounded closer. Desperation seeped from his voice. "Please, Davin, let her go. She doesn't want to be with you. She is with me now. We are married."

The words from Slater triggered Davin's anger even more, and he spat when he spoke. "Shut the fuck up, okay! You stole her from me."

Davin pressed his arm deeper into my neck, and I winced from the pain. "You are hurting me," I cried between coughs.

He tugged again as he glared at our friends, horrified and frozen with fear. "Shut up, Sabela." He hissed when he spoke, and his nostrils flared. "Sabela is mine, and she has always belonged to me. If anyone tries to stop me, I swear to god I'll kill her."

"Now, wait a minute," Slater yelled. "Don't you fucking hurt her!"

Davin yelled back. "Hey man, if I can't have her. I'm sure as hell not going to let you or anyone else have her."

My body was no longer trembling; it was shaking vigorously as I was being dragged away from the crowd. My mind raced with ways to escape, but I had no plan; I had no idea. I was in pain, and his hold on me was stronger than any strength I had inside of me to fight back. I tried to scream but couldn't. Tears gushed down my face. My mouth quivered, and I was petrified. I wanted to be safe in Slater's arms.

Within seconds, I heard the sound of running feet, and then Slater was standing in front of us. "You are not taking her anywhere," Slater ordered.

"Out of my fucking way, asshole. I'll break her fucking neck right here. Is that what you want?"

Slater pushed him hard on the chest with the palms of his hands. "Like hell, you will!" and then quickly reached in front of me and grabbed the cake knife from the table close by. The crowd screamed as Slater wasted no time and rammed the knife into Davin's chest. My body stiffened at the sight of the knife protruding from Davin's chest. I froze as his grip on me loosened. Davin gasped and held his chest as he began to fall to the floor.

The sound of a loud gunshot caused me to scream as I watched Slater hold his body and fall to the floor. "No!" I screamed. "Someone call an ambulance. Slater has been shot!"

Davin's limp body fell to the ground. Blood saturated the brown t-shirt he wore. One of his hands was still in his pocket that now bore a hole where he had been holding the hidden gun.

I raced to Slater's side and knelt beside him. "Hang in there, baby." I cried as I rested his head in my lap. Slater's body shook, and beads of sweat formed on his brow. His face winced as he tried to curl his body to ease the pain.

I looked up at the crowd, stunned by what they had witnessed. Cries and screams continued, and I yelled loud above the confusion to be heard. "Someone call a fucking ambulance." I made eye contact with my mom and Lorenzo, who were hugging the twins, and had Scottie standing close in front of them. "Mom, get the kids out of here."

I looked down at Slater. My body shook vigorously, and tears poured down my face. "It's going to be okay, baby." I reached down and saw Slater had his hand over his wound, but I could still see the blood. I wept and placed my trembling hand on his, and applied pressure. Blood seeped through the cracks of my fingers and over my skin.

I looked up when I heard a woman screaming and pushing herself through the crowd.

"This is all my fault. I'm so sorry."

Confused by her confession, I watched as Claire's mom, Abigail, collapsed on the floor next to Slater and buried her head in her hands.

"What are you talking about?" I said in a shaken voice between my tears—wondering what she knew.

Claire's father, Jeffery, was close behind. "Stop, Abigail." He shouted. "That's enough."

Claire, who was at my side, intervened and came between her mom and dad. "No, dad. I want mom to talk. What is this all about?" She looked down at her mom, who continued to cry hysterically. "Why is this mom's fault?"

CHAPTER 37

My eyes narrowed, and I glared at Abigail. "Talk to us, goddamn it! Your son is dead, and Slater is lying here with a bullet inside of him."

Abigail looked at me, and I sensed she was seeking forgiveness, but until I knew what was going on, I had none. She rocked her body with her hands held up in front of her face. Her voice was shaking when she spoke. "I tried to give up my son, but I just couldn't. I am his mother. How am I supposed to do that?"

"What are you saying, mom?" Claire said with an edge.

"Don't, Abigail," her father pleaded.

Claire quickly turned and hissed. "Shut up, dad. Let her talk."

Slater released an agonizing moan. I hugged him and stroked his damp forehead. "Tell us, Abigail," I yelled.

"I told Davin about the wedding. We never stopped seeing him."

Claire stepped away from her parents and shook her head. "What? How could you? You've been lying to me this whole time?"

Abigail reached out her hand towards Claire, but Claire pushed her away and found the comfort of Travis's arms.

"Please, Claire; It wasn't like that." Her mother begged. "At first, I only told him you were getting married and that I wished he could be there for his sister's wedding. I never mentioned Sabela or Jill, just you. I told him you were having a beach wedding and a nice reception at this restaurant." She bowed her head and became hysterical. "But the next time I saw him, I made the mistake of saying *the girls* had bought their dresses. He caught on right away and asked what I meant by *the girls*. He asked who the other girls were. What was I supposed to say? So I told him you were all getting married on the same day. He already knew where and when because I already told him during our last visit. I'm so sorry. Please forgive me."

I was stunned by what I was hearing, but had no time to digest it. Suddenly we were surrounded by police and an ambulance crew who immediately attended to Slater.

"Is he going to be okay?" I pleaded, with tears rushing down my cheeks as I moved away from Slater and into Jill's arms.

"We will know more when we get him stabilized and to the hospital. It appears to be a gunshot wound to the abdomen. As long as there are no injuries to his vital organs, he should be okay."

"Can I ride with him to the hospital?"

"Check with law enforcement, ma'am. They may want to keep you here for questioning."

I was the first to explain everything that happened to the police. I rushed my speech, and my heart raced as I watched Slater being lifted onto a gurney. "Please, officer. Can I be with my husband? They are taking him to the hospital. I need to be with him. We just got married. This was our wedding."

The officer glanced over at Slater and then over at Davin's now covered body. "Yes, you can go with him. I think I have everything I need from you. An officer will be at the hospital shortly to take a statement from your husband when he can."

"Thank you."

"We will be there as soon as we can," Claire shouted from a

chair nearby, where she huddled with Travis. Jill and Ricky stood next to them in each other's arms. "We will too." Ricky echoed.

I gave my friends a weak smile through my tears and took Slater's hand as they wheeled him out to the ambulance.

When we arrived at the hospital, Slater was immediately wheeled away. I wept as I watched the nurses push his gurney and race down the corridor through the double doors. I stood alone in the chilled corridor with no arms to fall into. I had no voice to tell me everything was going to be okay and to give me words of comfort. I now knew what Claire must have gone through while Travis was in a coma. I saw a row of seats against the wall and made my way over to them. After I set my purse on one of the empty chairs, I noticed the bloodstains on my dress for the first time and wept again. Was it Slater's or Davin's blood? I cringed at the thought that it might be Davin's and distracted my thoughts by hastily hunting for my phone buried in my purse.

After one ring, I heard the comforting voice of my mom. "Sabela. Are you okay? How is Slater?"

"I'm at the hospital, mom. I'm so scared. I'm waiting to hear from the doctors. How are my girls and Scottie?"

"They are okay, sweetheart. They are all asleep. Lorenzo and I have been sitting here anxiously, waiting for your call. I didn't want to call you. I have never been so scared in my life. I thought that man was in jail, and where did he get a gun? He could have killed you, Sabela. My god."

"I have no idea where he got the gun, mom."

My mom was as shocked and confused as me and had so many questions. "How did he know you were getting married today?"

"His mom told him."

"What? I thought they disowned him. Well, at least that's what Claire told me."

"That's what her parents told her. Look, mom. I'm sure we will find out more. I'm just finding all of this out. I'll call you as soon as I have any news about Slater. I love you. Kiss the kids for me."

"I love you too, Sabela."

I'm not sure how much time had passed before my phone rang and woke me. I didn't realize I had dozed off. I glanced at the screen and saw it was Claire.

"Hey, Claire."

"We are in the lobby. Where are you?"

I glanced around. "Some corridor. I have no idea where. Let me come to you."

When I walked through the double doors into the lobby, it warmed my heart to see Ricky, Jill, Travis, and Claire. I was also pleased to see Caroline, Travis's mom, with them too. They, too, were still dressed in their gowns and tuxedos. Their support is what I needed right now, and when I felt their arms around me, I felt at home.

"Any news on Slater?" Travis asked.

I shook my head as we stood in a circle in the waiting room. "No, not yet." My hands held together in a prayer, "Please let him be okay." The waiting room was quiet and brought back memories. "Last time we were here was when Travis was in a coma, and here we are again."

Jill released a slight chuckle and tried to perk up our broken spirits. "Yeah, we have to stop meeting like this, and twice in one year is enough."

We all smirked at her joke and took seats next to each other while still holding hands.

Claire sat next to me and squeezed my hand. "I'm so sorry, Sabela. I feel partly responsible. After all, it was my mom's stupidity that caused all of this."

Her words crushed me. I didn't want her to feel any guilt. "Please, Claire. You have nothing to do with this. How were you supposed to know that your parents were still seeing Davin?"

"I know, but I feel like I should have suspected something." Her eyes grew wide. "That's where they were when they went away on weekends. It makes sense now. They were visiting him. Davin was in some prison just outside Santa Clarita. It's a few hours' drive from here. They probably stayed in a hotel close by."

I was concerned about her now fragile relationship with her parents. "Do you think you will ever forgive them?"

She hesitated. "Let me ask you the same thing. Slater was shot. Will you forgive them?" She patted my hand. "Right now, I honestly don't know. It's too soon, Sabela. What I am concerned about is Slater."

She was right, and I smiled at her. "I'm sorry. I shouldn't have asked."

We spent the next few hours trying to keep our spirits high while we waited for news from the doctors. We listened to a comical story from Ricky and Jill about their first encounter in the very waiting room where we were seated. Ricky added some humor by reminding us how stubborn Jill had been and how it made him almost give up pursuing her. Jill reminded him he had given up, and if it wasn't for her seducing him in the shower, they might never have gotten together. Of course, we asked for more details about the shower, but Jill quickly waved off our request with a devious laugh.

Claire held me the entire time and comforted me when I would break out in tears when Slater's name was mentioned. I tried to stay focused on the stories being told and show a forced smile when needed, but after a few minutes the fears I had not knowing how Slater was doing haunted me. Fearing the worst, I broke down when I thought about his girls and Scottie growing up without him.

"He's going to be okay," my friends told me as I tried to hold it together.

"Well, we are about to find out. Here comes a doctor." Jill said as she pulled herself away from Ricky's arms and sat up straight.

CHAPTER 38

The middle-aged male doctor with white hair and silver-framed glasses approached our group and smiled. "I'm Doctor Westley, and I'm looking for Sabela Chester."

I raised my hand slowly. "That's me. We were married today."

The doctor released a slight chuckle. "I gathered that by the dress you are wearing." He glanced over at Jill and Claire, focusing on their dresses. "And you two also got married?"

Claire nodded. "Yes, we are all best friends and got married on the same day."

"How is Slater? Please tell me he is going to be okay." I shook my head, realizing they would have his real name. "I mean Ian. Slater is his nickname." I clenched my fists and held my breath while I waited for the doctor to reply.

He smiled, which eased me a little. "He is a very lucky man, and he is going to be okay. So sorry this happened at your wedding."

Everyone released a sigh of relief and echoed, "Thank god."

"He was shot in the hip area and had a flesh wound from the gunshot, and none of his vital organs were damaged. We removed the bullet successfully, and he is now recovering. The doctor's smile grew when he saw our bodies relax.

I clutched my heart. "Oh, thank god. When can we see him?"

"We are going to keep him for a few days, but I don't see any reason why you can't see him in a couple of hours. The police are going to see him shortly. After they have spoken to him, I'll have a nurse notify you."

A terrifying thought crossed my mind. "I hope they don't arrest him. It was self-defense. Davin had a gun."

Claire quickly stood and wrapped her arm around me. "Calm down, Sabela. I'm sure that won't happen. We all saw what happened and gave the cops our stories. They have no reason to arrest him."

I looked at Claire. "I hope you are right."

I shook the doctor's hand. "Thank you, doctor. I know you don't have the answer. Thank you so much for taking care of Slater."

A friendly redheaded nurse told us we could finally see Slater three hours later. They were the longest three hours of my life. They had no restrictions and allowed us all to go to his room. Apparently, Slater was doing well. He was experiencing some pain from the wound, which they gave him medication for. He was alert but feeling somewhat groggy.

I didn't know what to expect when I opened the door to his room and tiptoed in with the others following close behind. But as soon as I saw Slater's smiling face looking my way, all the fears I had been carrying for the past few hours quickly disappeared and were replaced with tears of joy.

Slater raised his arms slowly as I raced over to his side and perched on the edge of the bed. He moaned in pain, causing me to stand quickly.

"I'm sorry. Did I hurt you? I'm just so happy to see you."

"I'm okay, just a little sore." He patted the bed. "Come on, sit next to me. Just don't press up on my side. That's where I got shot."

I eased my body slowly onto the edge of the bed and leaned in gently to kiss Slater's lips. "I was so scared that I had lost you."

He brushed the hair out of my face and kissed me again. He spoke slowly from fatigue, and his eyes looked heavy. "I'm still here, baby. I'm not going anywhere. How are my baby girls and Scottie?"

"They are at my mom's. They are fine."

The others gathered around the bed, and each gave Slater a caring smile.

"You had us, scared, bro," Ricky said as he pulled Jill into his arms.

"Did you know that asshole had a gun when you stabbed him?" Travis asked.

Slater shook his head. "No. The cops asked me the same thing, and they said he was hiding it in his pocket."

I quickly changed the subject. I had concerns of my own I wanted answers to. "What did the cops say? They are not going to arrest you, are they?"

"They pretty much said it was an open and shut case of self-defense. Who knows what may have happened if he had pulled out his gun and opened fire." Slater stopped talking to catch his breath. "They actually commended me on my bravery. They were aware of Davin's record. This is what they know so far. Details are still coming in, and their investigation is still ongoing." He stopped and took another breath.

I rested my hand on his chest as he took some deep breaths. "It's okay, honey, take your time."

Slater nodded and held his wounded side as he spoke. "He somehow escaped from prison early this morning while on outside duty. A hole was discovered in one of the wire fences. They have reason to believe it was a deliberate escape, and a little of the fence was cut at a time so as not to be noticed. He had the tools needed while working outside."

"But how did he get the gun and change clothes?" Claire asked with a creased brow.

"The cops believe he stole a car from a couple at a gas station right off the freeway close to the prison. The prison is next to the freeway. He couldn't have picked a better car. The couple were gun enthusiasts from Oregon on their way to a gun convention in Los Angeles. From what the couple told the cops, the husband went inside to pay for the gas and grab some snacks. He had left the keys in the ignition because his wife stayed in the car, but she didn't see them when she went to use the bathroom." Slater stopped talking again to catch his breath and rest his head on his pillow. After some time, he continued. "Anyway, Davin wasted no time stealing the car and headed south to San Diego. They found the car a mile away from the restaurant where we were. The cops believe he found the handgun and bullets in their luggage and a change of clothes. They found two rifles and three more handguns when the car was searched. They were untouched."

Guilt swept over Claire's face again. "I'm really sorry, Slater. This is all my mom's fault: her and her big mouth. I'll never forgive her for this. I forgave her once, and she lied to me. How can I ever trust her again?"

Slater raised his hand on his good side. "Now hold on a second Claire. We can't forget that she was just being a mom. I know Davin was your brother, but I can't imagine the pain she felt when she saw her son in jail and the crimes he had committed. Like any mom, I'm sure she wanted to fix everything. I'm quite certain she didn't tell him in the hopes he would escape and try to kidnap Sabela. Her heart was crushed because her son was in prison. A son that is now dead. She was sharing with him a part of your life, her other child, and letting him know how sad she was that he wouldn't be there for your wedding day. From what I understand, the rest was told to him by accident, or Davin somehow coaxed it out of her."

Travis turned to Claire. His eyes were sad. "She's going to need you, Claire, and so is your dad. They lost a son today; it wasn't their fault. Davin died today because of what he did. They didn't tell you they saw him because they obviously were afraid they would lose you again. You can't blame them for that."

Claire folded her arms. "I just need some time. I know you are right. I'm all they have now."

Travis's mom smiled at Claire. "Sweetheart, I know this is really hard for you. I'm sure your mom regrets everything right now and believes she has lost her daughter again. I never thought I would ever see Travis. But I am here with him now because of you. Travis brought you and your parents together, and you thanked him. Even now, as you find it hard to forgive your mom, you know it was the right thing to do back then. Put yourself in your mom's shoes. Don't punish her for being a mom. Love her and be there for her and grieve the loss of Davin together."

Claire's mood quickly changed. "I could never grieve Davin's death. I'm sorry. He was a monster, and I feel no pity for him. Slater did the world a favor when he killed him. You are asking a little too much."

Caroline raised her hands. "I'm sorry, I take that back. But as a mom who has regretted giving up her son over thirty years ago, please don't give up on your mother."

Claire wiped away her tears. "Like I said, I need some time. I promise I will think about it."

Ricky tried to change the somber mood. "So, how are you liking married life, guys?" Ricky joked.

We all chuckled at his joke. "Well, that was a wedding to remember," Slater said while patting his wounded side. "Hey, aren't you two leaving for Vegas in the morning?" he added.

"We can't leave while you are laid up in the hospital," Jill protested.

"Why not? I'm fine." Slater insisted. "I'm going home in a few days. They just want to make sure there is no infection. What are you going to do? Sit around and watch Sabela change my bandages. This is your wedding day too. Please go to Vegas." he insisted.

Jill and Ricky looked at each other and then at all of us. "Really? You think we should still go?" Jill questioned with a furrowed brow.

I smiled and gave my head a hard nod. "Yes, Jill. You guys should go. You just got married, for god's sake, go celebrate. Be with your husband. Davin did enough to spoil our wedding. Don't let him ruin your honeymoon too." My heart embraced the thoughts I suddenly had. I turned to Slater and gave him a loving smile. "Thanks to my husband, Davin can no longer hurt any of us. I want you to celebrate not only your wedding but mine and Slater's too and also Travis's and Claire's. When you toast your love to each other, toast ours too." Suddenly, something occurred to me. "Hey, who will watch Maggie?"

Jill beamed a big smile and leaned into Ricky. "Sadie and Logan offered to watch her." She gave all of us a big smile. "Okay then! Vegas, here we come." She tugged on Ricky's arm. "Come on, babe, we are going to Vegas."

ABOUT THE AUTHOR

Tina Hogan Grant loves to write stories with strong female characters that know what they want and aren't afraid to chase their dreams. She loves to write sexy and sometimes steamy romances with happy ever after endings.

She is living life to the fullest in a small mountain community in Southern California with her husband and two dogs. When she is not writing she is probably riding her ATV, kayaking or hiking with her best friend – her husband of twenty-five years.

www.tinahogangrant.com